PONY in a PUMPKIN PA

DATE DUE 10/14

PONY in a PUMPKIN PATCH

by Ben M. Baglio

SCHOLASTIC INC.

New York Toronto London Auckland Sydney
Mexico City New Delhi Hong Kong Buenos Aires

ISBN 0-439-87117-4

12 11 10 9 8 7 6 5 4   7 8 9 10 11/0

Printed in the U.S.A.   40
First Scholastic printing, October 2006

Special thanks to Andrea Abbott

PONY in a PUMPKIN PATCH

One

"Golden eagle!" Mandy Hope exclaimed.

The huge shadow skimming across the ground was unmistakable. Mandy wound down her window and leaned out of the Land Rover. "There it is!"

The eagle was swooping toward a stretch of water not far from the road. The map of Scotland on Mandy's lap showed that this was Loch Long, one of the many narrow freshwater lakes found in this country. The distinctive, straight-sided stretches of very deep water had been carved out during the Ice Age, when massive glaciers flowed down from the mountains to the sea.

Mandy's dad, Dr. Adam Hope, pulled over to the side of the road and looked out, too. "Just look at that wingspan. It must be six feet across at least."

Gliding swiftly on its outstretched wings, the eagle was soon just a speck above the glassy waters of the loch. "That was amazing," Mandy said. She picked up a brochure on the seat next to her. The title read ARGYLL FOREST PARK. Below the heading was a photograph of a golden eagle.

"We're lucky to have seen one so quickly," her dad commented, driving on again.

They'd only just arrived in Argyll Forest Park, a vast wilderness of mountains, valleys, and forests in the southwest of Scotland. Looking down at the map, Mandy saw that two lochs, Loch Eck and Loch Goil, reached deep into the park, nearly dividing it into quarters. Two others, Loch Long in the east and Loch Fyne in the west, framed the park on either side. There was water everywhere!

Mandy turned to the back of the brochure where there was a list of Scottish wildlife. Taking a pen out of her pocket, she checked off "golden eagle." "One down, lots more to go! I can't wait to see red squirrels and red deer," she said. She'd read in the pamphlet that Scotland had the biggest populations of these species in the whole of the British Isles: three hundred thousand deer, and a little more than a hundred thousand squirrels. There were very few red squirrels left in the rest of Britain because they'd been displaced by the greedier, more aggressive gray squirrel that had been introduced from America.

"Rollo's promised that both squirrels and deer are on the sightseeing agenda," said Dr. Adam.

Rollo McCruish, an old school friend of Mandy's dad, was one of the forest rangers in Argyll Park. He and his wife, Cara, had invited the Hopes to spend the October school break vacation with them. They lived on a privately owned estate within Argyll Park called Longshadows. Mandy's mom, Dr. Emily Hope, was unable to join them because she and a cousin had already booked a week's break at a spa. So Mandy and her dad had come to Scotland on their own.

Mandy glanced out the window again. They were driving along the top end of Loch Long, which, true to its name, was long and finger shaped. "I wonder if there's a Loch Long monster to check off?" she joked, thinking of the very famous Scottish monster, Nessie, that was said to live in Loch Ness farther to the north. From time to time, newspapers carried reports of people claiming they'd seen an enormous, prehistoric-looking animal in the loch. Sometimes there were even photographs of strange-looking shapes in the water, but these usually turned out to be hoaxes. Some people were just too eager to believe the monster myths!

Dr. Adam looked at Mandy. "Haven't you heard about Longie?"

Mandy wrinkled her nose. "Longie?"

"First cousin of Nessie," said Dr. Adam. He pretended to look shocked. "My own daughter has reached the age of twelve and she hasn't yet heard of Longie! Whatever do they teach you in school these days?"

"Not to believe wild stories." Mandy laughed. "And really, Dad, couldn't you have come up with a better name than Longie?"

"Like what?"

Mandy stared out the window again. "Like . . . like . . . *squirrel*!"

"Squirrel? That's a strange name for a monster," said Dr. Adam.

"No, a squirrel, really. A red one. In that pine tree! Stop, Dad!"

Dr. Adam braked. "Just as well there aren't other cars behind us. We'd drive them crazy with all this sudden stopping and starting."

"Shh, Dad," Mandy whispered. "It'll hear you."

The russet-colored squirrel was scurrying along a branch of a tall spruce tree about ten yards from the road. It was small and lightly built — not as stocky and round as the gray squirrels Mandy knew so well. It had large ear tuffs that seemed almost too big for its head, and its delicate fluffy tail curved over its back. Mandy thought it was one of the cutest animals she'd ever seen, especially when it stared down at the Land Rover and nibbled a pinecone that it held in its tiny front paws.

After a while it seemed to grow tired of being a tourist attraction. *Chuk-chuk, chuk, chuk,* it chattered, annoyed, and it dropped the chewed pinecone onto the ground before scurrying higher up the tree.

"Bye-bye, and have a good day, too," laughed Dr. Adam, starting the engine again.

The road soon veered west away from the loch. On either side, the forest grew thicker. Mandy peered into the trees, looking for signs of life. She was crazy about animals — *all* animals. And with her parents being vets, she even lived at a veterinary practice! Their clinic was called Animal Ark, and it was attached to their stone cottage in the Yorkshire village of Welford.

After a few miles, Mandy's dad left the main road by a signpost that read LONGSHADOWS. "Here we are," he said. "I'm dying for a cup of tea." It was late afternoon and they'd been on the road since breakfast, stopping only once for lunch.

A sweeping driveway took them through a beautiful country estate. Tall trees grew in ornamental groves surrounded by checkerboard-smooth emerald-green lawns. "Is this the McCruishes' front yard?" Mandy wondered aloud. Even though she knew their home was on the Longshadows estate, she'd imagined a forest ranger would live in a small wooden cabin hidden among the trees!

A very different type of house came into view around a bend. "They live in a mansion!" Mandy gasped.

Dr. Adam laughed. "I don't think Rollo would agree with that." He turned onto a narrow gravel road that ran beside the imposing gray stone house. "Rollo and Cara live in a cottage on the estate," he explained, driving through an open gate marked PRIVATE. "An old Scottish family — the Buchanans — owns the main house. They live in one wing and the rest is open to the public. If you're interested, we could take a tour one day."

"That would be great," Mandy said.

They drove into a neat gravel yard behind the main house and parked in front of a whitewashed building. It was single story with sash windows and a two-part wooden door in the center. Mandy thought it looked a lot like a stable.

A short, broad-shouldered man with curly black hair came out to meet them. "Adam, Mandy!" he said, his warm smile making Mandy feel instantly at home. "Welcome to Argyll Forest Park."

"Good to see you, Rollo," said Dr. Adam, climbing out of the Land Rover.

"Did you have a good trip?" Rollo asked.

"It was wonderful," Mandy said, jumping down from the passenger side. "We saw a golden eagle and a red squirrel."

"That makes it a great trip," agreed Rollo.

The men carried the luggage to the cottage. "I hope you don't mind sleeping in a stable," Rollo warned as they went inside. "This used to be the stable for the big house."

Mandy's first impression had been right! "A converted stable? I couldn't think of a better home." She caught

her dad's eye. "Except for a cottage with a veterinary clinic attached to it," she added with a grin.

"We'll leave your things here for the time being," said Rollo. The tiny hall was already crammed with water-proof clothing, boots, and walking sticks. "Tea's ready. I'm sure you're dying for a cup."

"My words exactly." Dr. Adam smiled.

Rollo pushed open a latched wooden door leading into the living room. To Mandy's delight, there were still traces of its original purpose. "I can see where the stalls used to be," she said. The dividing walls had only been partly demolished, leaving several waist-high ledges jut-ting out from the back wall. The spaces between these ledges would have been where the horses were teth-ered on deep straw beds. Now they formed several alcoves, one making a sitting area with plump sofas and chairs placed around a fireplace, another the dining area, and a third an office with a desk and computer.

On the wall above the computer, Mandy saw a gilt-framed painting of an enormous red stag with a mag-nificent set of antlers. Standing on a hill, against a backdrop of rugged mountains, the powerful stag gazed loftily at the world around him. "What a beautiful pic-ture!" Mandy said. "He's like a king looking down on his kingdom."

"That's what he is, in a way," said her dad. "The

painting's called 'Monarch of the Glen,' and it's by a nineteenth-century artist called Sir Edwin Henry Landseer. It's one of his most famous animal portraits."

"Of course, this isn't the original," Rollo said hastily.

"Tea's ready," came a voice from the other end of the room. Mandy saw a petite woman coming through an archway. She was about the same age as Mandy's mom and had thick dark hair that tumbled around her shoulders. She was carrying a tray piled high with tea and snacks.

"Cara! How good to see you again," said Dr. Adam, going over to kiss her cheek. He took the tray from her and set it on a low table.

"It's good to see you, too, Adam and Mandy," said Cara. She gave Mandy a friendly smile. "Welcome to our humble home. And please, take a seat." She gestured to the sofas.

"It's not humble at all," Mandy said, sitting next to her dad. "I'd love a cottage like this."

"You must be a horsewoman if your ideal home is a stable," Cara said, chuckling.

"Not exactly," Mandy said. "I ride whenever I get the chance, but I don't have my own horse."

"If you love horses and you ride, that makes you a horsewoman," said Rollo. He poured the tea while Cara passed around the snacks.

Dr. Adam helped himself to a chocolate brownie. "Mmm," he said, biting into it. "You could give my mother a run for her money, Cara." Grandma Hope was famous in Welford for her baking.

"I get lots of practice, that's all," Cara said modestly. "I've been running the tearoom at the main house for the past few months."

"When can I start looking for red deer?" Mandy asked, hoping she didn't sound too impatient.

"How about tomorrow morning?" Cara offered. "We could go out for a ride together." Mandy's face must have lit up because Cara quickly added, "I can't offer you a horse, I'm afraid, but we do have mountain bikes."

To Mandy, the prospect of riding through Argyll Forest on a bike to look for deer was almost as appealing as going on horseback. "I'd like that a lot," she said.

"Am I invited?" asked Dr. Adam.

"Sorry, there are only two bikes," Rollo told him. "But you could join me on a patrol of the Ben Donich area to monitor some deer tomorrow. There have been a lot of sightings of big stags hanging around herds of females there."

"Sounds good," said Dr. Adam, helping himself to another brownie.

Mandy frowned at him, knowing her dad was always trying to lose weight.

"If I've got to hike up a rugged Scottish mountain and stalk large stags that are protecting their lady friends, I need to build up my strength," he said, grinning.

"Rest-And-Be-Thankful," Mandy read, getting off her bike next to a signpost at the side of the road. "That can't be a real place, can it?"

It was just after nine the next morning. Mandy and Cara had been cycling for about twenty minutes up a steeply winding road through a valley called Glen Croe.

"It's actually a flat area at the top of this road," said Cara, jumping off her bike as well. "On a clear day, it has an amazing view across the valley."

Mandy followed the twisting road with her eyes. She figured they had at least halfway to go, and the road just seemed to get steeper and steeper.

"The plateau was called Rest-And-Be-Thankful because before there were cars, travelers were very grateful to get to the top of the pass and see that the rest of their journey was downhill," Cara explained.

"I bet they were," Mandy agreed. She gazed around at the backdrop of towering peaks. Sheets of dark purple heather covered the rolling hillsides. Far below, a river snaked through the valley, disappearing whenever it met a dark green patch of forest but emerging again on the other side, an unstoppable silver thread. Even though Mandy was used to the wide-open spaces of Yorkshire, the scale of this scenery made her feel very small.

They climbed back on their bikes and pressed on. Soon Mandy found herself crouched over the handle-bars, breathing hard. She turned her head quickly and looked over the edge of the road. The vehicles on the road that ran along the valley looked like toy cars.

About 150 feet ahead of Mandy and Cara, there was a small farm nestling beside the road. A half dozen cows and a small flock of sheep grazed in a stone-walled paddock behind the cottage. In front of the cottage and at the sides, the ground was thickly planted with vege-tables. One of the fields next to the cottage was dotted with bright orange globes: pumpkins, Mandy guessed. They looked rather startling against the muted palette of purple, brown, and green that covered the rest of the landscape.

"Do you know who lives there?" she asked Cara when she had enough breath to speak.

"Mr. Nesbitt," answered Cara. "He grows the best vegetables I've ever tasted. Oh, there he is."

A man was coming out of the cottage. His arms were

raised like he was waving to someone. "I think he's seen us," said Cara. "Let's go and say hello."

They had gone only a few yards when Mr. Nesbitt shouted, "Get out!"

Mandy was a bit taken aback. "Does he mean us?" she asked Cara.

"I don't think so. We're not even on his property yet."

"Get out!" Mr. Nesbitt shouted again. A gust of wind muffled his voice, and Mandy heard only snatches of what he said next.

". . . ruined . . . disaster . . . out of there!"

"Something's wrong." Cara sped up. "We'd better find out what it is."

Mandy pedaled faster to keep up. They had just started bumping down the track that led to the farm when a jet-black pony appeared from behind the cottage and cantered straight past Mr. Nesbitt, into the pumpkin patch.

"Get out of there!" the farmer yelled, and he set off after it, waving frantically.

A sturdy fence blocked the pony's path. It whirled around and charged back through the pumpkin patch, only to come up against a stone wall. It stood there, stiff-legged and wide-eyed, its tail swishing uneasily. Mandy realized it was soaked, as if it had been in a rainstorm — and yet there'd been no rain. There was also frothy white foam in its mane and tail. Something very odd was going on!

Mr. Nesbitt strode toward it, still waving his arms.

"We've got to help that pony. It's terrified!" Mandy cried. She pushed down on the pedals as hard as she could. She had to reach the frightened pony before it hurt itself!

Two

Mandy threw the bike into a hedge and scrambled through the fence. The pony was just a few yards away, wild-eyed and frightened, surrounded by bulging pump-kins and knee-deep in green vines. Even though the pony was rigid with fear, Mandy could see that it was beautiful. Its coat was jet-black, its eyes a warm brown color like melted chocolate, and there was a perfect white star on its forehead.

Mandy walked forward slowly. "It's all right, I won't hurt you," she said soothingly.

"Catch it, quick!" cried Mr. Nesbitt, scrambling through the vines. "And watch where you walk!"

Mandy glanced around at the bulky orange pumpkins lurking among the heart-shaped leaves. Some of them were enormous, perfect for carving at Halloween! She didn't think she'd damaged any, but she winced when she saw two squashed ones in front of her, scarred with unmistakable horseshoe-shaped dents.

"Get that pony out of there!" Mr. Nesbitt ranted. "And make sure it doesn't get into my potatoes and cabbages, too."

"OK," Mandy said, wishing he'd stop shouting. She understood he was worried about his pumpkin crop, but shouting would only make the pony more upset.

There was a gate farther along the wall, and a dark green van was parked in the driveway on the other side. There were several pumpkins in the back, and a half dozen others in a wheelbarrow next to the gate.

"Would you stay back, please? We don't want to make the pony feel crowded," Mandy called to Mr. Nesbitt.

Cara was also working her way across the pumpkin patch. She stopped when Mandy called out.

Mandy continued toward the pony. "You're safe now," she promised.

Gradually, the little horse seemed to grow calmer. It stopped swishing its tail and blinked at Mandy as she came nearer. Mandy saw she was a mare in tip-top condition. Her eyes were bright and her coat, although soaking wet, was thick and glossy.

When she reached the pony, Mandy stretched out her hand. The mare sniffed her fingers, her puffs of breath like a warm breeze on Mandy's palm. "Good girl," she whispered. Gently, she grasped a handful of foamy mane. "Shall we go now? Before we squash any more pumpkins?" She took a step toward the gate and clicked her tongue. "Come on, girl."

The pony started to follow Mandy. "That's it," she said and walked on more quickly.

Moments later, they were out of the pumpkin patch and on the other side of the wall. Mandy steered the pony clear of the wheelbarrow so that no more pumpkins were damaged. Farther along the drive, she stopped next to a wind-bent tree and put an arm around the pony's neck. "We can take you back to your paddock now. But what gave you such a scare? And why are you soaking wet?" If only animals could talk!

Mr. Nesbitt and Cara came through the gate.

"Well done, Mandy," said Cara.

The farmer nodded. "Thank you, lass."

"I'm glad I could help," Mandy said.

Mr. Nesbitt looked much calmer now. He was wearing a tweed flat cap, baggy gray pants, and a thick navy-blue sweater that looked rather moth-eaten. There were leather patches on the elbows where the wool must have worn away. He took off his cap and wiped his forehead with the back of his hand. "You saved the day, young lady. My pumpkin crop could have been ruined."

"What was the pony doing in there?" asked Cara.

"I was loading the van," Mr. Nesbitt explained. "I went inside to answer the phone. But, fool that I am, I left the gate open. I looked out of the window and saw the pony cantering down the drive straight for the pumpkins. So I ran out and . . . well, I think you saw the rest."

Mandy was still stroking the mare. "What gave her such a scare?"

Mr. Nesbitt shrugged. "I don't know."

"Maybe we should get her back into her paddock before anything else happens," Mandy suggested. "If you tell me where it is, I'll lead her there."

Mr. Nesbitt shook his head. "She's not mine. I don't know where she came from. When I saw you chasing after her, I thought she must be yours."

"I'm afraid she's not," said Mandy ruefully. She'd love to own such a beautiful pony. "Do any of your neighbors have horses?"

"Only Margie McFadden," answered Mr. Nesbitt. He pointed to a grassy peak about a mile above them. There was a tiny white cottage near the top. "But this pony doesn't belong to her," Mr. Nesbitt went on. "Her horse is a big brown fellow. Even a rocket wouldn't make him gallop off like this pony did."

Cara stroked the pony's flank, looking thoughtful. "I wonder if she comes from that yard on the other side of Rest-And-Be-Thankful? There's a place on the road to Loch Fyne where they breed Dales ponies. She looks a lot like the horses I've seen there."

Mandy took a closer look at the mare. Her mane was very long, hanging below her neck, which was solid and naturally arched. Her tail was also longer than most breeds of pony, sweeping the ground in soft black waves. "She does look like a Dales pony," Mandy agreed. She'd seen ponies like this at the Walton Show. "What a coincidence!" she said. "We're both from the Yorkshire Dales, yet we bump into each other hundreds of miles away from home!"

The pony shook her head and snorted.

Mr. Nesbitt looked nervously at the mare, glanced back at his precious pumpkin crop, then at the pony again. "Now you mention it, she does look like the ponies at Loch Fyne." He ran his hand over his thinning gray hair. "It's the Nelsons' place, isn't it?"

Cara nodded.

"I don't go that way very often," the farmer said meaningfully. "I don't suppose . . ."

"That we could take the pony there?" Mandy guessed.

"Yes," said Mr. Nesbitt. "You see, I've got all these pumpkins to deliver. With it being Halloween this week, everyone wants a pumpkin! But if you're not going that way . . ."

"Oh, but we are, aren't we, Cara?" Mandy said.

"Yes, we were heading in that direction. I guess we can just as easily go on foot with a pony in tow." Cara smiled.

Mr. Nesbitt looked relieved. "Thank you." He replaced his cap and frowned at the pony. "She'll need some sort of bridle."

"A rope will do," Mandy said confidently.

Mr. Nesbitt raised his eyebrows. "Are you sure?"

"She's calm now," Mandy said. The little mare seemed to have forgotten whatever it was that had spooked her. She was nudging Mandy's hands for treats, her whiskers tickling Mandy's fingers.

"I'll see what I can find." Mr. Nesbitt hurried away, returning a minute later with a coil of thick, slightly oily rope.

Mandy twisted it into a halter using a knot her best friend, eleven-year-old James Hunter, had taught her. He would love to be here helping with such a gorgeous pony! He was almost as crazy about animals as Mandy was. Between them, the two friends could have written a book on all the animal experiences they had shared.

Mandy slipped the halter over the pony's head. "Ready, girl?"

Mr. Nesbitt offered to put their bicycles in his shed, and Mandy and Cara set off down the road with the pony walking between them.

"How far is it?" Mandy asked. She was walking at the pony's shoulder, holding the halter just below the pony's head in one hand, and the end of the rope in the other. The mare stepped out eagerly, her ears pricked. Her coat was drying now, but there were still traces of foam in her mane. Her tail hung in thick damp curls, and Mandy's fingers itched at the thought of combing it until the hair fell like spun silk.

"About a mile," replied Cara. She looked at her watch. "I hope this doesn't take too long. I've got to open the tearoom at eleven thirty."

They got on the road again and continued up the steep pass to Rest-And-Be-Thankful. The traffic was heavier now so they kept to the grassy roadside, out of the way of passing cars. Mandy kept her fingers crossed that the vehicles wouldn't unsettle the pony.

But the mare wasn't fazed at all by the cars and trucks. The only time she seemed anxious was when a

motorbike roared past with a large Union Jack flag fluttering cheerfully on the back. The pony flattened her ears and sidestepped so that she bumped against Mandy, but settled down when the bike disappeared over the top of the hill.

"I don't blame you for shying away from that noisy machine," Cara sympathized, stroking the pony's neck.

At the summit, Mandy looked back the way they'd come. "No wonder this place is called Rest-And-Be-Thankful," she remarked. From here, she could see how steep the road really was!

To keep with tradition, and because they were a bit out of breath after their long climb, they sat down to rest on the heather-covered ground. "The hard climb is worth it, though," Mandy said. She could make out Mr. Nesbitt's farm below them, and even saw his green van turn onto the main road before heading east along the valley.

They let the pony nibble the grass next to the parking area for a few minutes before they started down the other side. After about a mile, they came to a wooden sign at the start of a trail. LOCH FYNE STABLES, it read. Underneath the words there was an elegant carving of a pony with the same flowing mane and tail as the mare's.

"Let's hope this *is* where you come from, little pony," said Cara.

The trail took them through a gate toward a cluster of stone buildings. The pony whinnied and walked faster. Mandy started to feel more hopeful. Did the mare recognize where she was?

Wood-fenced paddocks lined the drive on either side, and in each, several ponies looked up curiously at the procession going past.

"Look at those ponies!" Mandy exclaimed. "We must be in the right place." Just like the runaway mare, the ponies had thick, dark-colored coats and flowing manes and tails, while the hair on their lower legs and fetlocks was long and full. "Do you know the owners of this horse farm?" Mandy asked.

"I've met them a few times," said Cara. "They're named Zoe and Kenneth Nelson. They have twins, Zachary and Faye. They're about thirteen, I think."

Mandy couldn't help envying the twins. "Imagine owning so many beautiful ponies and being able to ride every day! I'd never sit down, except when I was in the saddle," she joked.

"Well . . ." Cara began as they entered the stable yard.

She was interrupted by a voice ringing out from a corner. "There you are!"

Mandy looked around. A girl was propelling herself across the gravel yard in a wheelchair.

"Hello, Faye," said Cara. "So this *is* your pony?"

"Hi, Mrs. McCruish," replied Faye. "Yes, this is Jewel."

"Jewel!" Mandy echoed. "That's a perfect name for her."

Faye pulled up next to them and flicked on the brake to stop her chair from rolling forward.

"This is Mandy Hope," said Cara. "She's staying with us for Halloween."

"Hi, Mandy," said Faye. She looked up at Jewel who lowered her head and blew gently into Faye's hair. Faye leaned back, laughing. "Bad girl, running off like that," she said. "Where did you find her, Mrs. McCruish?"

"At Mr. Nesbitt's farm," Cara explained. "Mandy managed to lead her out of the pumpkin patch before she did too much damage to the Halloween crop."

"Oops!" Faye gulped. "That would have been terrible." She smiled at Mandy. "Thanks for bringing her home. Zach and Mom are going to be so relieved. She broke loose and galloped out of the yard when Zach was washing her."

That explained Jewel's soggy coat, and the soap bubbles in her mane and tail.

"She hates being washed that much?" Mandy said in surprise.

Faye let off the brake and rolled forward, then bent down to run her hands over Jewel's front legs, checking them for injury. "Actually, she never objected before," she explained, wheeling around to check Jewel's hind legs. "But she can be a little nervous. She seemed tense right from the start, and when a horse blanket blew across the yard that must have been the last straw." She gave Jewel a gentle pat on her flank. "You're OK, girl. Let's get you into your stable."

She wheeled herself forward and was about to take the rope from Mandy but seemed to change her mind. "Would you like to lead her in, Mandy, since you two have hit it off so well? Her stable's the one at the end. Next to my pony." She nodded to where a gray pony with a white blaze was peering over a stable door.

"What a beautiful pony!" Mandy gasped.

"She's the best," Faye said proudly. "Her show name is Loch Fyne Fairy Glen, but we just call her Glen."

As Mandy started toward the stables, a boy dressed in grubby denim overalls jogged into the yard. Mandy guessed it was Zach because he was practically a carbon copy of his sister. They both had green, almond-shaped eyes, chestnut-colored hair, and the same dazzling smile.

"Great! She's back!" Zach exclaimed. "Did you find her, Mrs. McCruish? You and . . . er . . ."

"Mandy," Faye told him. "She and Mrs. McCruish found Jewel in a pumpkin patch."

"A pumpkin patch?" Zach frowned as he came over to give Jewel a pat. "What were you doing there, hmm?"

"Trampling them, I bet," said Faye. "Now, you'd better hurry, Zach, if we're to make the show in time."

Mandy pricked up her ears. "You're going to a show?"

"*Supposed* to go. This afternoon in Dunoon. I'm riding Jewel in the M and M class," said Zach, taking the rope from Mandy.

"M and M? For Mountain and Moorland?" Mandy checked.

Faye looked impressed. "You know about Mountain and Moorland ponies?"

"A little," Mandy told her. "I know they're native British breeds, originally semiwild ponies that were bred on mountains and moorlands."

"For someone who claims not to be a horsewoman, you know a lot about ponies," said Cara.

Mandy shrugged. "Not as much as Zach and Faye, I bet. There are Mountain and Moorland classes every year at our local show. What I love most about them is the way the ponies are kept so natural."

"Yes, not groomed to perfection!" Zach grinned. He led Jewel to a hose in a corner of the yard.

"That's the way I like ponies to look, too," Faye agreed, spinning her chair around and following her brother and

Jewel. "No braided tails and manes, or pruned coats that make them look like performing poodles!"

Mandy and Cara walked along next to her.

"This is a really important show for us," Faye went on. "It's one of the last chances to qualify for the Scottish Championships next month."

Zach was waiting with the hose. "No pressure," he joked, but Mandy could tell he was nervous from the creases in his forehead.

"I'll keep my fingers crossed for you," Mandy told him.

"Thanks," said Zach. He turned the faucet on and began rinsing out the foam in Jewel's tail.

Cara checked her watch. "We ought to be on our way, Mandy. I've got to be at work soon."

"Oh, right," Mandy said, trying not to show how disappointed she was that she couldn't stay longer.

"Would you like to come to the show with us?" asked Zach.

"I'd *love* to," Mandy replied. She turned to Cara. "Do you mind?"

"Of course not."

There was just enough time for Mandy to go back with Cara to get her bike from the farm. Then Cara set off down to the valley while Mandy headed back to the yard.

She paused briefly at Rest-And-Be-Thankful to get

her breath back before starting downhill, changing gears as the hill grew steeper. Soon she was freewheeling in top gear, with the wind blowing in her face. On either side, the Highland landscape whizzed past in a blur of green and brown.

She slowed down as she approached a bend in the road. A movement in some trees not far ahead had caught her eye. A pair of dark brown shapes was emerging from the trees.

"Oh, wow!" she whispered, braking sharply. "Red deer!"

They were both stags, their powerful necks surrounded by thick manes, almost like a lion. They each had the most amazing antlers, the spreading horns reminding Mandy of trees in winter.

She was just thinking how lucky she was to have seen them when a loud guttural roar splintered the air. It was so unexpected that Mandy jumped. A second roar answered the first. In the blink of an eye, the stags spun around to face each other and . . . *Clash!* Two sets of antlers collided with a hideous, rattling crack, sending shivers through Mandy.

"No!" she said, gasping. How could the deer have been walking calmly together one minute, and fighting the next?

The stags pulled apart, one backing up a few paces.

Clash! Again, the stags lowered their heads and locked antlers, the sharp-pointed tines hooking together. They stayed with their heads down, entangled, for a few seconds before one stag suddenly twisted his head free. Mandy expected him to run off but instead he butted the other stag again.

Stop it! Mandy screamed silently. She couldn't bear it if one was hurt.

The stags pushed into each other until one started to force his opponent backward. The defeated stag wrenched his antlers away, then whirled around and charged back into the forest. The victor chased him a short distance before stopping to let out a triumphant roar. *And don't come back!* he seemed to be saying.

Mandy realized she was shaking. She waited a few minutes until the winning stag moved away into the trees. Then she climbed onto her bike and pedaled unsteadily away, the sound of the clashing antlers echoing in her mind.

Three

Fifteen minutes later, Mandy raced into the stable yard. She was afraid watching the stags might have made her late for the horse show. To her relief, the Nelsons hadn't left yet. A trailer was hitched to the back of a Land Rover in the middle of the yard. Faye was just wheeling herself into Jewel's stable, and Zach was peering into the back of the Land Rover. "Where's the traveling blanket, Mom?" he shouted.

Mandy saw a blond-haired woman with the same green eyes as the twins coming across the yard. She was carrying a tweed riding jacket on a hanger. "I don't know!" she called to Zach. "Try the tack room." She sounded rather flustered but she smiled when she noticed Mandy. "You must be Mandy. Thank you for bringing Jewel home."

"No problem," Mandy said, puffing, breathless from her high-speed ride. She leaned the bike against the wall. "I hope I haven't kept you waiting."

"Don't worry, we're not quite ready to go," said Mrs. Nelson, leaning across the backseat of the Land Rover to hang up the jacket.

"I took longer to get back because I came across two stags fighting," Mandy continued.

Zach was opening the back of the trailer. He stopped and looked at Mandy. "Awesome!"

"It was. But scary, too," Mandy confessed. She went to help Zach with the ramp.

Faye came out of the stable, leading Jewel behind her. She'd looped the lead rope around her wrist so that she could push herself forward with both hands. "Did you say you saw stags fighting, Mandy?"

"Yes. I was so worried they'd get hurt," Mandy replied.

When Faye came close to Mandy, Jewel stretched out her neck to nuzzle Mandy's hand. She seemed to recognize her already! With her black coat gleaming and her mane and tail brushed, Mandy thought she looked more gorgeous than ever.

Mrs. Nelson patted Jewel. "OK, let's get her loaded."

"Have you found the traveling blanket yet?" Faye asked Zach.

"I was just going to look for it in the tack room," he said, jogging across the yard. He came back with a sky blue cotton blanket edged in dark blue. The Loch Fyne logo, a silhouette of a Dales pony with LOCH FYNE STABLES below, was embroidered on one corner. Zach threw the blanket over Jewel's back, and Mandy helped him to fasten the straps.

"All set now," Zach said, taking the reins from Faye. "In you go, Jewel."

Mandy patted her on the shoulder to encourage her to go in. Jewel walked calmly up the ramp and into the box.

"She loads beautifully," Mandy said. "When I think of how scared she was earlier, it's hard to believe this is the same pony."

"She's a little like a Jekyll and Hyde character," said Faye. She had wheeled herself to the Land Rover and, with her mom's help, was pulling herself into the front passenger seat. "One minute she can be as good as gold, and the next she'll be acting up."

Zach came back down the ramp, and Mandy went to help him lift it up.

"Just a minute," he said. "The chair has to go in, too." He got the wheelchair, folded it up, and lifted it into the trailer. He rested it against the wall on the other side of the partition from Jewel and fastened two canvas straps around it to keep it still.

"That's everything," he said, pushing his cap back off his forehead. "Let's go."

Mandy and Zach closed the trailer and climbed into the backseat of the Land Rover behind Faye and Mrs. Nelson. There was a lurch as they pulled away and then they were driving down the lane on their way to the show.

The road to Dunoon, where the show was being held, followed the eastern shore of Loch Fyne for about ten miles before turning east at the village of Strachur. From there, it cut back through the edge of Argyll Forest Park. Five minutes later, they were driving along yet another finger-shaped stretch of water.

"This loch's even narrower than Loch Long," Mandy noticed.

"It's Loch Eck," said Mrs. Nelson.

Faye twisted around in her seat. "Not far to go now. Are you still nervous, Zach?"

He shrugged and looked out the window. "No . . . well, um . . . kind of."

"I bet you'll be great," Mandy said, meaning it. She looked out of the back window. She could see Jewel's lovely face with its white star through one of the glass panes at the front of the trailer. *I wonder if she's nervous, too?*

When they reached the show ground, Mandy sensed the excitement even before she climbed out of the Land Rover. Brightly colored banners and streamers decorated the rings, while one section of the ground was crowded with stalls selling tack and other horse equipment, as well as a range of hot snacks like pancakes and ham sandwiches. Riders in neat black jackets and spotless cream jodhpurs hurried purposefully between the parked trailers and a row of official-looking tents. Mandy couldn't help envying them. It must be amazing to compete in such an important event.

Best of all, there were horses everywhere — warming up, being groomed, or waiting patiently beside their trailers. Mandy could see almost every breed she'd heard of, from long-legged thoroughbreds with their manes tightly braided to tiny ponies being ridden by equally tiny riders. "I've never seen so many amazing horses in one place!" she exclaimed as she jumped down from the Land Rover.

"You must have," said Faye. She'd opened her door and was waiting while Zach got her chair. "You said you have a horse show every year where you live."

"It's nothing like this," Mandy said, admiring a

magnificent chestnut cob. The rider, an elderly man, greeted the Nelsons with a nod of his head.

"What kind of show is it?" asked Faye.

"A general agricultural show with dog classes as well as horse classes, and lots of livestock," Mandy told her. "There are tents for handicrafts and vegetables and things like that, as well."

"That sounds like fun," said Mrs. Nelson, helping Faye down.

"It is," agreed Mandy. She stood back to make room for the wheelchair.

Mrs. Nelson lifted Faye into the chair then pointed to a blue tent. "Faye, will you and Mandy fetch Zach's number from the secretary's tent, please, while we unload Jewel?"

"Will do," said Faye. She pushed forward, greeting people who waved to her. It seemed to Mandy as if everyone knew everyone else in the horse world!

They got Zach's number from the secretary's tent — a big black 8, printed on a piece of cream card that Zach would tie to his waist. As they headed back to the trailer, they saw a tiny cream pony being led by a neatly dressed woman. The rider, a little girl, looked as if she was barely four years old, but she sat up straight and held the reins confidently in her gloved hands. She looked very professional in a tailored navy jacket, yellow jodhpurs, and short leather boots. An emerald-green ribbon in her hair matched the color of the woman's outfit. She saw Mandy and Faye and waved to them. "Hello!" she called. "Mommy, there's Faye."

"Hello, Bonny," Faye replied, adding, "good afternoon, Mrs. Byrne," when Bonny's mother looked around and waved, too. "They're competing in the First Ridden Pony class," Faye told Mandy. "That's how I started out, on the smallest pony you've ever seen. He was called Nelson's Touch, and he was great in the ring but could be incredibly naughty outside!"

Mandy was surprised to hear that Faye had ridden once, but she kept the thought to herself.

Another pony caught her attention, a striking dapple gray being led out of a trailer in the parking lot. "He's beautiful!"

"That's Marble Arch," said Faye. "He's a Connemara, which is an Irish breed. He's Jewel's hottest rival."

"In what way?" Mandy asked. Marble Arch was stunning, but so was Jewel.

Faye put her hands on the wheels to stop the chair. "To start with, he has excellent conformation." She watched the pony's rider walk him around. "And he moves like a dream. One of the things the judges look at is a pony's paces, how smoothly it walks, trots, and canters."

"Jewel moves beautifully," Mandy said loyally.

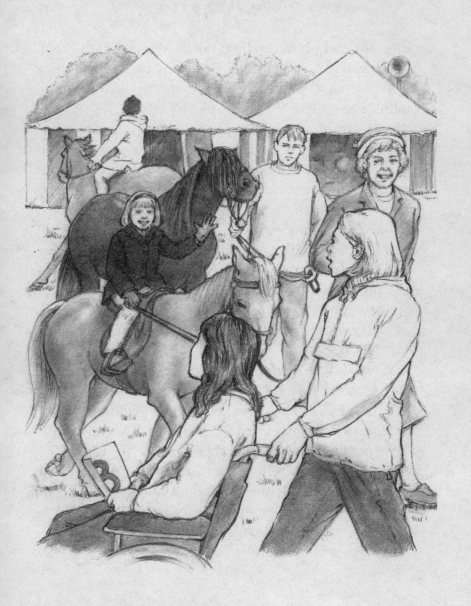

"She *is* good," agreed Faye. "But Marble Arch really daisy cuts when he gets going."

"Daisy cuts?"

"Sweeps the grass with the tips of his hooves," Faye explained.

"And Jewel doesn't?" Mandy asked.

Faye wheeled herself forward again. "It's not a characteristic of Dales ponies. They tend to have a choppier stride, lifting their knees higher than a breed like the Connemara, which has Arabian ancestry. If a judge prefers smoother paces, they'll probably place Marble Arch above Jewel."

Back at the trailer, there was no sign of Zach and Mrs. Nelson.

"They must be warming up," said Faye. She sat up and peered to the far side of the trailer park. "There they are, in the practice ring."

Mandy and Faye weaved their way through the trailers to the warm-up area. Zach was trotting Jewel in circles. Mandy hardly recognized him. Instead of grubby overalls, Zach wore cream jodhpurs, gleaming ankle-high boots, and a perfect-fitting tweed jacket over a yellow shirt and green tie. He pulled up next to Mandy and Faye to take his number.

"You look ready as ever," Mandy said. She patted

Jewel's neck, and the pony swung her head around to snuffle Mandy's hair.

"Thanks," said Zach. He tied the number around his waist. "Our class is in the main arena," he said. "The one with all the blue banners at the entrance."

Mandy saw the sponsor's banners bulging slightly in the gentle breeze, advertising a major bank.

Zach and Jewel went back to warming up. Mandy noticed that Mrs. Nelson looked tense. Her arms were folded and she bit her bottom lip as she watched the pair trot around the ring.

"Is there a problem?" Mandy asked quietly.

Mrs. Nelson shrugged. "I hope not. But Jewel's edgy. Look at her tail."

Mandy saw that it was clamped down, in the same way a nervous dog might hold its tail down tightly.

"Her ears are back, too," Faye pointed out. "She must be in a bad mood."

"That's all we need," said Mrs. Nelson. She motioned to Zach. "Bring her over. I want to—" She was interrupted by an announcement over the loudspeakers.

"Class twenty-four is about to start. Large Ridden Mountain and Moorland to the main area, please."

"That's us!" Faye exclaimed.

Four

Mandy felt a flutter of excitement when Zach and Jewel entered the ring. Jewel's ears were still back and her tail was clamped down, but Zach seemed to be doing his best to reassure her. He spoke to her constantly, and stroked her neck as they walked past the steward into the ring. The judge stood in the middle, watching the ponies as they walked around the edge of the arena. Jewel was fourth from the front, behind a handsome bay roan. Marble Arch and his rider were three ponies behind Jewel, looking very poised.

Outside the railings, Faye was parked next to Mandy. She leaned forward in her chair, biting her nails. Mrs.

Nelson stood on the other side of Faye with a box of grooming equipment and a folded horse blanket at her feet.

"See what I mean about Marble Arch?" Faye told Mandy. "He's in a class of his own."

"So is Jewel," Mandy said, because Jewel had started to look a lot more relaxed. Her ears pricked up and her tail flowed gracefully behind her. Perhaps being with the other ponies had helped calm her down.

The steward pointed his whip at the lead pony, a chestnut mare. She broke into a trot. The rest of the class took their cue and changed pace, too.

Jewel settled into a steady trot, with her neck arched and her mane flicking up at the ends. "She looks great, doesn't she?" Mandy commented.

"Much better," agreed Mrs. Nelson. "If they keep this up, we could have a chance."

The steward pointed his whip at the lead pony again. The class changed direction, trotting across the ring from one corner to the other. Mandy rested one foot on the lower rail and folded her arms on the top one. Suddenly, a gust of wind snatched the map out of her hands. It fluttered to the ground just inside the ring. Mandy ducked under the rail and grabbed it before it could be blown farther in. When she stood up, her heart skipped a beat.

Instead of trotting in line with the other ponies, Jewel was sidestepping across the ring with her head up and her tail swishing anxiously.

Mrs. Nelson looked dismayed. "What on earth does she think she's doing?"

And then, to Mandy's horror, Jewel put her head between her knees and started kicking her hind legs up in the air. Zach sat very still, leaning back as she bucked beneath him.

"She's going to bang into the other ponies!" cried Faye.

Zach shortened the reins and tried to push her forward, but Jewel bucked again, and Mandy saw Zach lose one of his stirrups.

"What's the matter with her?" Mrs. Nelson said.

Mandy was just as puzzled. She was also very worried about Jewel. The pony was acting as if she'd seen a ghost!

The steward walked briskly over to Zach. Stonefaced, he said a few words and strode away again.

"They've been told to leave the class," Faye said gloomily.

"Oh, no!" Mandy bit her lip as she watched Zach dismount and lead Jewel out of the ring with his head bowed in disappointment.

"She was doing just fine!" Zach said, throwing his hard hat into the back of the Land Rover. He took off his jacket and flung it onto the seat.

"Hang that up, please," said his mom, who was tying Jewel to a metal ring on the side of the trailer.

Zach muttered something under his breath and leaned across the seat to reach the hanger.

"Maybe she's not feeling well," Mandy suggested, studying the pony's face for a sign that she might be a little ill.

Jewel gazed back at her without giving any hints about how she was feeling.

"It can't be that," said Mrs. Nelson. "We had her checked by the vet yesterday to make sure she was one hundred-percent. He called in to see one of our brood mares, so I had him take a look at Jewel, too." She took off the saddle and put it on the grass, propped against the wheel of the trailer.

Faye took a body brush from the grooming kit and started to smooth out the marks left by the girth. "He said she was in excellent shape."

"She's not sick," Zach agreed. "I just don't think she can handle big shows. The noise, the crowds, the size of the ring — it's too much for her. She really freaked out in there. It's not worth putting her through it again."

Faye stopped grooming Jewel. "But this is her first major show!"

Zach frowned. "So?"

"We can't expect her to behave perfectly the first time," Faye argued. "She's young and has a lot to learn. You can't blame her for being skittish today."

"I'm not blaming her," said Zach. He rubbed the mare's nose. "You're just not cut out for this kind of thing, are you?" he asked her.

Mrs. Nelson took the traveling blanket from the trailer

and draped it over Jewel's back. "Well, let's hope for better luck next time. We'll go home and start preparing for the next show."

"There isn't going to be another one," Zach announced.

"Yes, there is," Faye told him. "There's one more chance to qualify for the championships next weekend, remember?"

"I know," Zach said impatiently. "But we're not going to qualify if she behaves like this again. So there's no point in going."

No one spoke much on the drive back to Loch Fyne. Even the sight of a pair of red squirrels running along the telephone wires couldn't cheer Mandy up. Zach's pessimistic words kept ringing in her ears.

When they arrived at the yard, Zach didn't wait to help with Jewel. He stomped straight into the house, pausing only to take off his boots at the kitchen door. Mandy helped Mrs. Nelson lead Jewel out of the trailer and into her stable, while Faye followed behind with the grooming kit on her lap.

"I'll let you two do it," Mrs. Nelson said. "I should call Dad," she told Faye, "to let him know how we did."

"My dad's in New York on business," Faye explained

to Mandy when Mrs. Nelson had left. "He's going to be really disappointed when he hears what happened."

Jewel started eating her feed at once — proof, Mandy thought, that she was feeling fine inside. But there were signs that she'd been under stress; patches of dried sweat clung to her coat where she hadn't been brushed yet, and the muscles at the top of her tail were still very tense.

Mandy and Faye began grooming her. "Too bad Zack doesn't want to go to the next show," Mandy said after a while. She stood back to admire the pony. Brushed and buffed, Jewel gleamed like a black pearl. "Jewel is so beautiful!"

Faye nodded. "I think so, too. And, deep down, so does Zack. But you heard him. He's nervous about what Jewel might do. He doesn't want to take any chances."

"But he's such a great rider," Mandy protested. A less talented rider might have fallen off when Jewel acted up in the show ring, or couldn't have stopped her from bumping into the other ponies.

"Yes, he is. But . . ." Faye glanced through the door. Apart from the trailer and Land Rover, the yard was empty. "Zack lost his nerve a year ago, after my accident," she explained quietly.

"Oh! I'm sorry, I didn't know," Mandy said.

She must have looked shocked because Faye quickly said, "No, *I'm* sorry. There's no reason you should have known. I don't talk much about the accident."

Mandy wasn't sure what to say next.

"It took Zach a long time to get back into a saddle," Faye went on.

"I suppose I can understand that," Mandy said, trying to put herself in Zach's shoes. She wondered if a skittish pony had caused Faye's accident. That would explain why Zach didn't like Jewel leaping about.

Faye continued. "Glen — that's my pony, remember?"

Mandy nodded, picturing the gray pony with the white blaze she'd seen looking over her stable door.

"She's usually very reliable, but one day last autumn, during the grouse-shooting season, we were out trail riding and a gun went off nearby," Faye recalled. "Before I could do anything, Glen bolted." She paused and looked away fleetingly before picking up the story again. Her voice sounded very calm and matter-of-fact, as if she wasn't describing something that had dramatically changed her life. "We went over the edge of a quarry. It was a big fall to the bottom — at least thirty feet. Zach raced after us and found us lying in a heap on the ground."

Mandy gulped.

"Glen broke her leg but she managed to pull through," Faye went on. "And I, well . . . I broke my back. The doctors did everything they could and I was in months of rehab. But hey!" she said with a look of determination. "It could have been a lot worse. We're both lucky to be alive."

Lucky to be alive! Mandy was in awe of Faye's courage. She must miss riding so much. And how tough to have to be reminded of what she had lost every single day.

Faye's voice cut into Mandy's thoughts. "I know what you're thinking."

"I, er . . ." Mandy began.

"And no, I don't miss riding."

"You don't?" Mandy asked, surprised.

"Not at all," Faye chuckled. "Because I still ride."

Mandy was even more surprised. "How?"

"We had a special saddle made for me," explained Faye. "I'd never give up riding. Not for anything. It's my life."

The sound of footsteps outside made them both look around. Zach appeared in the doorway. "Look, I didn't mean that about not going to the next show," he said, coming in. "You're right, Faye. Jewel is young and she still has a lot to learn." He put his arms around the mare's neck and hugged her. "You just need some time to get used to big shows, don't you? We'll give you another chance on the weekend."

"Great!" Mandy exclaimed.

Faye looked relieved, too. "You know what I think we should do before the next show?"

"What?" asked Zach.

"Go out trail riding," his sister replied. "It might take Jewel's mind off whatever spooked her today."

"Good idea," said Zach. "Let's go tomorrow." He looked at Mandy. "I hope you're coming, too."

Mandy was thrilled to be invited. "You bet I am!" This vacation was turning out to be one of the best ever. She was actually going to have a chance to ride a gorgeous Dales pony!

Five

Cycling back from Loch Fyne twenty minutes later, Mandy noticed an old, crooked signpost about half a mile down the road. She'd missed it that morning on the way back to Mr. Nesbitt's place because she and Cara had been in a hurry.

The sign had a picture of a bicycle and the words LONGSHADOWS $1\frac{1}{2}$ MILES. Mandy guessed it was a shortcut back to the house. Although she didn't mind the climb up to Rest-And-Be-Thankful, it was getting late and she didn't like the idea of finding her way back in the dark.

Minutes after turning onto the path, she wondered if she'd made the right decision. The trail was deeply rutted and full of potholes, alarmingly steep in places and with tight turns on the downhill sections. Changing to the lowest gear, Mandy stood up and pedaled hard until she was back on level ground.

"That's better," she muttered, picking up speed again.

The easy ride was short-lived. After crossing a bridge over a stream, the trail entered the forest. The densely planted pine trees blocked out the rays of the setting sun so that it was almost pitch dark.

I hope it's not much farther, Mandy thought. The gloom made it difficult to pick out the path, and to spot obstacles like rocks and fallen branches. Mandy was forced to slow down. *At this rate, I won't get back till midnight!* She pressed on, hoping to see the welcoming glimmer of lights.

But it wasn't a light shining through the trees that caught her attention; it was a herd of deer. Approaching a clearing, Mandy saw them at the same time that they looked up and saw her. She braked gently so she wouldn't startle them.

The herd peered at her warily. Unlike the fighting pair Mandy had seen earlier in the day, these deer had no antlers. *That means they're all females*, she realized.

She remembered what Rollo had said about stags hanging around herds of does at this time of year. She

glanced over her shoulder and caught her breath. A stag was standing less than 30 feet behind her. He must have stepped out from the trees after she'd ridden past. Like the females, he stood still, staring at her.

It felt awesome to be this close to such a magnificent wild animal. But it was also a bit nerve-racking. The stag was enormous, over three feet tall at the shoulder. Like the pair Mandy had seen earlier that day, his neck was thick and covered in a shaggy mane. His antlers

were massive, too, but unlike those of the other stags,
his didn't have lots of branches. There were only two
main stalks, growing out on either side of his head.

That's strange, Mandy thought. The stag's coat was a
dull ginger color, very different from the rich dark
brown of the other stags. And his face seemed longer
than theirs, with closer-set eyes.

A rustling noise made her look in front again. The
herd was moving off, into the cover of the forest. "Sorry
I disturbed you," Mandy murmured. She turned her
head. The stag had vanished. Mandy was free to go on.
But what a privilege to have been surrounded by so
many red deer!

When she pedaled into the gravel yard in front of the
McCruishes' cottage a short time later, she saw her dad
looking anxiously out the front door.

"There you are!" he exclaimed. "I was about to send
out a search party."

"Sorry, Dad," Mandy said, pulling up in front of him.
"I was held up."

Before she could tell her dad about the deer, Cara
and Rollo came out.

"Did you get lost?" asked Rollo.

"No. I took a shortcut," Mandy said, jumping off
the bike.

"The trail through the forest?" asked Cara.

Mandy nodded.

"That's a tough ride," said Rollo.

Mandy wheeled her bike toward the garage. "Actually, it was great because I practically bumped into a herd of deer. The stag was there, too. And he had really weird antlers."

"Really?" said Rollo, sounding interested.

Mandy described the antlers, as well as the stag's long face and gingery coat.

"Those are all signs of an old stag," Rollo said, as Mandy leaned her bike against the garage wall. "I think I know which one you're talking about. He's at least thirteen years old, but he's still very possessive over his herd."

They started back to the cottage.

"You're very lucky to have seen him and his herd so close," said Dr. Adam. "We only spotted a small group in the distance."

"They're not the only ones I saw," Mandy said, wiping her shoes on the front door mat. "I came across two stags fighting."

"You *have* been lucky," said her dad.

Mandy followed the others inside. "I never imagined how big stags were or how strong."

"Well, they are Britain's biggest wild animal," said Rollo, opening the door to the living room.

"I was surprised when they started fighting," Mandy

went on. "When I first saw them, they were walking side by side like the best of friends."

"We call that parallel walking," said Rollo. "You're right, it does look like they're out for a friendly stroll, but stags often do that when they're about to get stuck into each other."

Cara was closing the drapes. "You've had quite a day, Mandy," she said. "What with rescuing a pony from a pumpkin patch, watching stags jousting, and going to a pony show. How did Jewel do?"

"Not very well." Mandy described what had happened. "It was awful for the Nelsons. But there's another chance for them to qualify next weekend."

"Let's hope things go better for them then," said Cara, heading for the kitchen. "Now, let's have dinner. You must be starving."

"I am," Mandy admitted. A delicious aroma drifted out from the kitchen, making her mouth water. "That smells good," she said, taking her place at the circular dining table.

"It's that world-famous Scottish dish, and one of my favorites: haggis," announced Dr. Adam, his eyes twinkling. "Which is sheep guts mixed with oatmeal and stuffed into a bag made from the sheep's stomach." He licked his lips in anticipation.

Mandy hoped he was teasing. She was a vegetarian, and the thought of guts and a sheep's stomach was enough to take her appetite away completely.

When Cara came in carrying a covered dish, Mandy studied it suspiciously. What if it really *was* haggis? At the risk of offending Cara, she'd have to refuse it.

"Ah, the haggis!" exclaimed Dr. Adam.

Across the table, Rollo picked up his knife and fork. "Let the feast begin!"

"Oh, stop teasing, you two." Cara chuckled. She took the lid off the casserole and Mandy sighed with relief. No bulging gray sheep's stomach, just some delicious-looking stuffed pasta tubes sizzling in the dish.

"Spinach and feta cannelloni," said Cara.

"One of *my* favorites," Mandy said in relief, giving her dad a playful nudge in his ribs.

To Mandy's delight, Jewel seemed happy to see her when she arrived at the stable the next morning. The pony pricked her ears and snorted as Mandy cycled in.

"Morning to you, too," Mandy said, laughing. She reached over the stable door to stroke her. In return, Jewel nibbled her sleeve.

"That's her way of showing affection." Faye smiled. She was sitting in front of Glen's stable, holding the pony's reins. Glen was already tacked up and stood patiently next to Faye's wheelchair, resting her muzzle on the back. "You're a big hit with Jewel," Faye remarked.

Mandy rubbed the mare's nose. "She's a big hit with me, too."

"So that means you'd be happy to ride her today?" said Faye.

"Really?" Mandy was stunned by the offer. "I don't know if I'm good enough."

Zach appeared from the tack room, carrying a saddle. "Of course you are. Jewel loves trail riding so you don't have to worry about her acting up."

The mare was nuzzling her neck now, her whiskers tickling Mandy's skin. "I'd love to ride her, thank you," she said.

She tried to ignore the butterflies in her stomach as she led Jewel out of her stable and helped Zach tack her up. "Who are you riding?" she asked, smoothing the leather guard over the girth buckles.

"Loch Fyne Printer's Apprentice," he said.

"Otherwise known as Peanut." Faye grinned.

"Nice name," said Mandy.

"Nice pony, too," said Zach. He went to a stall three doors down and brought out a strong-looking brown pony. At about fourteen hands, he was the same height as Jewel. He was saddled up already with the stirrups set high for safety. Zach pulled them down so that they hung level with Peanut's belly. "He's only five, a year younger than Jewel, and newly broken in," he explained. "But in a few years we'll be doing cross-country competitions together, won't we, Peanut?"

Mrs. Nelson came out from the house. "All ready?"

"Uh-huh," said Faye, handing Glen's reins to Mandy. "Hold on to her for a minute, please," she said.

Mrs. Nelson and Zach lifted Faye out of the wheelchair and into the saddle. Mandy noticed that it was shaped differently from regular saddles, much higher in front and behind so that the rider would be propped upright. She handed the reins to Faye then mounted Jewel. Alongside her, Zach swung himself onto Peanut's back.

"Have a lovely time," said Mrs. Nelson.

With Zach leading, they rode out of the stable yard, the ponies' hooves ringing over the pavement.

Mandy glanced at Faye. She seemed completely at home in the saddle, handling Glen with the kind of confidence that came from years of riding.

"Have you had Glen long?" Mandy asked.

"She was born here," replied Faye, ducking under a

branch. "Two years before I was born, which makes her fifteen. I started riding her when I was nine, so we've been partners for a long time."

Partners. Mandy thought it described Faye and Glen perfectly. They'd been through a terrible experience together and seemed all the closer because of it.

They rode up to a wide bridle path that cut across open fields. "Let's go!" Zach shouted, nudging Peanut into a canter.

Mandy leaned forward, gently pressing her heels against Jewel's sides. The pony hardly needed any encouragement. She lengthened her stride at once, breaking into a smooth gallop.

"This is fabulous!" Mandy shouted. She felt as if they were flying! Only the rhythmic drumming of three sets of hooves reminded her that they were still in touch with the earth.

Next to them, Faye and Glen kept up the pace. Faye's eyes were shining, and her long hair escaped from her ponytail and whipped across her face.

They raced on until the path narrowed and they were forced to slow down. "That was great!" Mandy said breathlessly as Faye pulled Glen up next to her.

"We'll have another chance for a canter later," said Faye. "Once we leave the forest, we go around the bottom of the Rest-And-Be-Thankful pass, then along the road to another flat stretch of grass."

"Do we go near Mr. Nesbitt's farm?" Mandy asked.

"Yes," said Zach, who had twisted around in his saddle to join in the conversation.

"Now I understand how Jewel ended up there the other day," Mandy said. "I suppose she knows this trail really well."

"Like the back of her, uh . . . hoof." Zach grinned.

They fell into single file as the path entered the forest. Here, the trail was strewn with pine needles that softened the thud of the ponies' hooves. A bird flapped out from a tree and across the path, startling Mandy. Jewel must have felt her reaction because she sidestepped briefly, but she calmed down when Mandy sat still and tightened her hold on the reins.

Mr. Nesbitt's cottage came into sight a few moments after they emerged from the forest. Mr. Nesbitt was in his garden carrying a huge pumpkin to his wheelbarrow. He smiled and called out to them, "Hello, there! Ready for Halloween?"

"Oh, no!" Faye exclaimed. "I'd completely forgotten about it."

"Well, you'd better start making plans. It's the day after tomorrow," Mr. Nesbitt reminded them.

"We will," said Zach.

He slowed down to let Mandy and Faye catch up with him. "I can't believe we haven't done anything about Halloween," he said.

"Do you go trick-or-treating?" Mandy asked.

"We would, if we had any close neighbors," chuckled Faye. "Do you?"

"Oh, yes. My friend James and I visit pretty much everyone in Welford, where we live. We usually end up with more candy than we can eat!" Mandy said.

"Trust the English to steal all the best Scottish traditions," Zach teased.

"But Halloween's not Scottish. It's American!" Mandy pointed out.

"Actually, it was Scottish people who took it to America," said Faye. "Halloween is based on an ancient Celtic harvest festival, Samhain."

"But it's such a big thing in America," Mandy protested. "It's hard to believe they didn't invent it there."

"Well, they added traditions of their own," Faye admitted. "Like carving pumpkins. That wasn't a Celtic tradition. The Celts carved turnips instead."

The trail merged with a narrow road. The three friends fell into single file, keeping close to the shoulder. For a change, Faye and Glen went in front.

"Why don't you come around and see us on Halloween

tomorrow night?" said Zach, who was riding just behind Mandy. "We'll show you all the Scottish traditions."

"I'd like that," Mandy said. Ahead, she saw Faye approach a sharp bend in the road.

"When we get home we'll figure out exactly what —"

Mandy never heard the rest of what Zach was saying. Without warning, Jewel reared up. Caught off balance, Mandy nearly fell off backward. "Whoa!" she cried.

Jewel's front legs flailed in the air. Her hooves brushed against a sheet of plastic that was flapping on the fence. It ripped in half, the torn-off piece floating away in the wind.

Jewel's front feet crashed to the ground. She backed up, her ears flat.

"Steady!" Mandy begged. She shortened the reins and gripped Jewel's sides with her knees.

But Jewel whirled around and reared up again, leaping into the middle of the road.

Screech!

There was the scream of slammed brakes, then the sound of a blaring horn.

Jewel didn't slow down.

Mandy closed her eyes, waiting for the sickening thud.

Six

Hooves clattered on the road beneath Mandy. Something brushed against her leg. The reins jerked in her hands. Then . . . nothing.

Was that it? Had they been hit? She opened her eyes.

Zach was next to her on Peanut. He held Jewel's reins in one hand, and Peanut's in the other. The car was at the side of the road, its engine stalled. Behind the wheel, the driver sat wiping his forehead. He looked shocked.

"That was close," said Zach. He was shaking, and his face was ashen. "Are you all right, Mandy?"

"I, uh . . . yes," she said, unable to control the tremor in her voice.

Faye had turned around. She stared at Mandy and Jewel, her eyes wide. "Phew! You're OK!" she gasped.

The driver climbed out of his car and walked over to Mandy. "You nearly caused an accident," he said angrily. "What do you think you were doing?"

Mandy swallowed hard and bit her lip. "I wasn't doing anything. Jewel just suddenly reared up. She must have gotten spooked."

"Over what?" demanded Zach. "There's nothing here."

"It's almost like she saw a ghost," said Faye, echoing Mandy's thoughts the day before.

"Ghost? Nonsense," said the driver. "Too much Halloween on your minds. That horse is obviously unsafe. She shouldn't be out on a public road." He got back into his car.

Despite her jangling nerves, Mandy came to Jewel's defense. "She's not unsafe," she protested. "She's just —"

"Plain dangerous," Zach finished as the man drove away. "The man's right. You could have been badly hurt, Mandy. Jewel shouldn't be on the road. Or anywhere else." He led the mare and Mandy back to the side of the road. Once there, he didn't let go of the reins.

"What do you mean, 'anywhere else'?" There was a sinking feeling in Mandy's stomach.

"She was OK all the way here," Faye pointed out, pulling Glen up next to the others.

"That's the whole point," said Zach. "You get no warning at all. It's a good thing you're a good rider, Mandy." He urged Peanut forward and tugged Jewel's reins. "Come on. We'd better get back before Jewel causes any more trouble. She's too dangerous to ride."

"I'm sure she'll be fine now," Mandy insisted.

Zach shook his head. "You don't understand. She can't be ridden anymore. Not at all."

"What about the show?" Mandy said, gasping.

"Forget about the show," said Zach. "Let's just concentrate on getting you home safely."

On the way home, no one said anything more about Halloween, or the show. And even though Jewel couldn't have behaved better the whole way, no one suggested that she deserved another chance.

But Mandy still believed in the gorgeous mare. Cycling back to Longshadows after the ponies had been turned out into their paddocks, she kept replaying the incident in her mind. There had to be a logical explanation for it. Again and again, she went through what had happened — in the pumpkin patch, at the show, and on the road.

She was so lost in her thoughts, she missed the bicycle trail to Longshadows. It was only when she found herself climbing up to Rest-And-Be-Thankful that she realized she had taken the longer route. She didn't pause to rest at the top; heavy black clouds were gathering and mist shrouded the valley below. *It looks like rain*, she thought, starting down the other side.

At the bottom, she found herself pedaling into the wind. She put her head down and pushed on, hoping she'd make it back to the cottage before the clouds burst.

Clap! Something like a gunshot rang out right next to Mandy. She jumped. Beside her, a pair of birds flew up in alarm, and a flock of sheep sheltering behind a stone wall bolted across the field. Mandy braked to see what had happened.

Crack! Clap! It was a large tarpaulin covering a hay stack. One of the ropes had come loose so that the thick plastic sheet billowed out like a sail, cracking sharply with each gust of wind. To the sheep it must have looked like a scary monster looming after them. "Poor babies," Mandy said, watching them scattering.

She started to pedal on, then braked sharply. "That's it!" she cried.

In a flash, everything fell into place: Faye said Jewel had bolted when a horse blanket flapped across the yard; a sheet of plastic flapped on the fence just before Jewel took fright that afternoon; and at Dunoon, sails and streamers had been flapping around the arena. Even the flag on the back of the motorcycle had made Jewel jumpy. Jewel is afraid of flapping things!

Mandy wanted to turn back right away to tell the Nelsons. But the rain was beginning to pelt down and she was closer to Longshadows than Loch Fyne. *I'll call them from the cottage*, she decided.

By the time she reached the cottage, Mandy was soaked to the skin. She burst into the kitchen. "Can I use your phone?" she asked Cara who was stirring something in a saucepan.

Cara looked taken aback. "You're drenched! You'd better change first."

"But it's really urgent," Mandy said. "I think I know what's making Jewel so nervous!"

Cara pointed to the phone in a corner of the kitchen. "Help yourself, dear."

Mandy picked up the receiver. "Oh, do you know their number?"

"I'll look it up." Cara paged through the telephone directory and read out the number.

Zach answered almost immediately. Mandy outlined her theory. "It's *got* to be that," she finished. "If you think of each time she's acted up, there's always been something flapping nearby. All we have to do is get her to accept things that flap."

"It does make sense," Zach admitted. "But the wind blows — things flap all the time. We can't start panicking every time it gets windy."

Mandy glanced out of the window. The rain was tapering off. "Look, why don't I come back to your place and we'll talk about it?"

"Lunch first," said Cara, motioning to the steaming pot on the stove.

"I'll be there as soon as I can," Mandy told Zach before she hung up and went to change. When she came back into the kitchen, her dad and Rollo were there. They'd spent the morning with officials from the Forestry

Commission to discuss ways of protecting red deer and
red squirrels.

"How was the trail ride?" asked Dr. Adam.

Mandy told him, trying to skim over the details of the
near accident. "We'll get Jewel through this," she con-
cluded confidently.

Dr. Adam raised his eyebrows. "Do you really think
you can straighten Jewel out in time for the show?"

"I'm not sure," Mandy admitted. "But Zach's on the
verge of giving up on her. I can't let that happen." She
finished her lunch — hearty vegetable soup and a home-
made bread roll, and pushed back her chair. "Would
you excuse me, please?"

"Sure," said Cara. "Oh, don't forget these." She gave
Mandy a bag of carrots for Jewel.

Mandy put the carrots in her coat pocket and started
toward the door.

"Are you taking the bike trail?" Rollo asked her.

Mandy turned around. "Yes."

"Then your dad and I might catch up with you. We're
going to look for that stag you saw yesterday," explained
Rollo. "The one with the killer antlers."

"Killer antlers?" Mandy echoed, taken aback.

"That's what we call antlers that have only the main
beams and no tines," said Rollo. "Another term is 'switch

head.' We usually see them on stags that aren't as dominant as they once were."

Mandy was puzzled. "Why call them 'killers' if the stag isn't as powerful anymore?"

Rollo took another bread roll. "When stags fight, the branches — or tines — make the antlers lock together. It's like a natural defense — full sets of antlers can't break through each other to hurt the stag. If there aren't any tines, the antlers can slide right through to the other stag. That's when you get fatal injuries."

Mandy thought of the majestic old stag she had seen. It was alarming to think he might cause serious damage if he got into a fight with another stag. Surely he would never intend to kill?

She got the bike and set off through the forest. Even though the path was even muddier after the storm, she barely noticed her tires slipping and spinning; her mind was buzzing with ideas to help Jewel. *We'll use her favorite treats to reward her when she does well*, she decided, pedaling up a short rise. *We have to convince her that good things go with flapping things!*

A loud barking interrupted her thoughts. It sounded like a big dog.

Then the barking gave way to a guttural roar. *Stag!*

She crested the rise and braked. The stag was just a

few yards in front of her, at the side of the path. At first, Mandy thought he was resting. He was lying in a clump of flattened shrubs, his head drooping in front of his chest.

But Mandy soon realized he wasn't asleep. He was breathing hard and his legs were crumpled awkwardly beneath him. Fearing he'd fallen and broken a leg, she craned her neck to get a better look. At the same time, the stag shifted his head. Mandy went cold.

His chest was covered in blood!

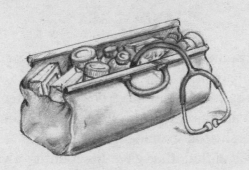

Seven

The stag caught sight of Mandy and tried to scramble to his feet.

Mandy felt a ripple of fear. She knew that injured wild animals could be unpredictable, even dangerous. She put one foot on the pedal in case she had to ride away quickly. But the stag slumped back among the bushes, too weak to stand up.

As quietly as she could, Mandy climbed off the bike and laid it on the ground without taking her eyes off the stag. She wished she could go over and comfort him the way she did with sick or injured pets. But it was different with wild animals. Their natural instinct was to

73

flee from humans. If they couldn't, they became very stressed.

A slight movement in the trees caught her attention. There was another stag standing about 50 feet from the path, watching the wounded deer.

It was his antlers that gave his identity away — they were sparse, with only the main beams and no tines. Killer antlers!

The old stag stood completely still. Had he seen Mandy? She wasn't sure. *I mustn't make any sudden moves.* She crouched down slowly in the shrubbery. All around her, the plants were broken and flattened, and the ground churned up. Perhaps badgers had been digging there or wild boars. A trail of pointed marks gave Mandy the clue she needed. Hoofprints. The two stags must have fought!

She stood up, forgetting not to move suddenly. She wanted to see just how badly the stag was hurt. Startled, the older stag whirled around and fled deeper into the forest.

The injured stag tried to get up again, but gave up almost immediately.

I've got to do something! Mandy felt desperate and powerless at the same time. She couldn't try to approach the deer in case she got hurt. *I'll go back for Dad and Rollo.* She started running back down the cycle path.

A few hundred yards down the trail, she heard the sound of an engine. Moments later, a Land Rover came around a bend not far ahead.

"Dad and Rollo!" Mandy gasped with relief. She ran toward them, waving frantically. When they pulled up in front of her, she yanked open the passenger door and scrambled inside. "Quick!" she panted, pointing up the path.

Dr. Adam looked worried. "What's wrong?"

"A stag's hurt," Mandy said. She leaned forward, peering through the windshield, as Rollo drove on.

A few moments later, she spotted the crumpled shape in the flattened bushes. "There he is!" she said, pointing.

Rollo cut the engine. "It looks like there's been a fight."

"That's what I thought," Mandy said. "The old stag was here earlier."

Rollo raised his eyebrows. "The one with the killer antlers?"

"Yes."

They climbed out of the Land Rover as quietly as they could, but their arrival clearly frightened the stag. He struggled to get up but failed just like before. Defeated, he collapsed back in the overgrowth.

"We've got to help him," Mandy whispered.

The two men exchanged a glance but said nothing.

Mandy felt her heart sink. She guessed they were going to say there was nothing they could do; that this was the way of the wild, and man should leave nature to take its course. It was an argument she'd heard often enough, and she understood it very well.

But that didn't mean she always agreed with it.

"I know it's hard to see an animal in so much pain," whispered her dad, as if he could read her mind. "But those injuries might be beyond our help already."

"We have to *try*," Mandy insisted.

"It's not that easy," said Dr. Adam. "We'll have to sedate him, then take him somewhere to treat him. There's also the park's policy to consider." He looked at Rollo. "What are the rules here concerning injured wildlife?"

"If I can help an animal without making things worse, I do," said Rollo. "Earlier this year, we rescued a doe that was trapped in a fence. We sedated her and treated her on the spot for an infection where the wire had cut into her neck. When she woke up, she seemed none the worse for the experience."

"So we *can* help the stag?" Mandy said eagerly.

Rollo shrugged. "It's a very different situation, Mandy. This fellow looks as if he's badly harmed. Like your dad said, we might not be able to do anything. And it's not just the injury I'm worried about, it's the shock. Handling him could make it even worse."

Mandy refused to give up. "If we leave him here, there'll definitely be no hope for him. So what's worse? Leaving him to die"— she hated having to say this out loud — "or doing what we can for him?"

The stag lifted his head and looked straight at Mandy. It seemed as if he was begging her to help him. "Please . . ." Mandy whispered.

Rollo studied the deer thoughtfully. "Maybe it's worth trying," he said at last.

Mandy closed her eyes with relief.

"But it won't be easy," Rollo warned. "He's a big guy — he must weigh at least three hundred pounds. We'd need to bring a trailer to take him to a forest station where we can treat him."

"We'll have to sedate him first," said Dr. Adam. "Otherwise he'll put up a big fight, which wouldn't do him any good."

Rollo sat back on his heels. "There are tranquilizers and other basic veterinary medicine at the cottage. If there's anything else we need, we can call our local vet."

"Or I might have them," said Dr. Adam. "I always carry my vet's bag with me." He looked at Mandy. "Don't get your hopes up too high, honey. I haven't had a chance to assess his injury yet."

Mandy nodded. "I know."

"OK. Let's get started," said Rollo, standing up. He climbed back into the Land Rover.

Dr. Adam got up, too, but Mandy stayed crouching in the undergrowth. "I'll watch over him," she offered.

Her dad's look showed he wasn't happy about leaving her there.

"It's all right, I'll be very careful," Mandy promised.

Dr. Adam frowned. "If the other stag returns, keep out of sight and stay absolutely still."

"I will," Mandy said.

"That old boy won't come back," said Rollo. "He knows he's won."

The men drove away, leaving Mandy crouched in the bushes. The wounded stag looked exhausted, his head hanging and his eyes closed.

"Don't give up," Mandy begged.

The stag must have heard her. He looked up and fixed her with a steady gaze.

"That's right," Mandy whispered to him. "You might have been beaten this time, but one day, you'll be in charge of your own herd."

As if he understood her, the stag straightened his neck. It was strong with a thick brown mane.

"You're absolutely magnificent!" Mandy gasped under her breath. His massive, many-branched antlers looked like a crown. He reminded Mandy of another stag she'd seen, the one in the painting in the McCruishes' living room — Monarch of the Glen.

"That's what I'll call you," Mandy decided. "Monarch. Because you *will* be a king one day."

The stag blinked. Mandy hoped he was agreeing with her.

About half an hour later, she heard the welcome sounds of an engine, and a trailer rattling noisily over the ruts in the track. "They're back," she said. "We're going to take you somewhere safe now, Monarch."

The stag must have heard the engine, too. He looked around nervously, and when he saw the Land Rover appearing over the hill, he panicked again. He kicked out his back legs, struggling to stand up. Mandy thought for a moment that he might succeed. He levered himself onto his front knees and was halfway up when he collapsed to the ground again.

"Quick, Dad!" Mandy begged as Dr. Adam and Rollo jumped down from the Land Rover. "We need to sedate him before he hurts himself any more."

Dr. Adam opened a first-aid box in the back of the Land Rover and briskly prepared a tranquilizing dart. He gave it to Rollo.

A *snap* echoed through the trees, and the stag slumped onto his side.

His three rescuers sprang into action. Rollo opened

the back of the trailer and let the ramp down while Mandy and her dad carried the first-aid box over to Monarch.

While Dr. Adam listened to the stag's heart and breathing, Mandy took off her coat and draped it over Monarch's head. "Just in case he's still aware of what's going on and can see us looming over him," she said as Rollo came across with a green plastic tarpaulin.

"Good idea," said Rollo. He spread the tarpaulin on the ground. "We'll drag him onto this then drag him to the trailer."

Dr. Adam cleaned Monarch's wound. "He's going to need a lot of stitches but they'll have to wait until we get him to the shed. I'll give him a shot of antibiotics now to stop any infection." He gestured to a syringe and a small vial in the first-aid box. Mandy handed them to him.

The next step was to load Monarch onto the trailer. As Rollo had predicted, the stag was very heavy.

"Definitely more than three hundred pounds," puffed Dr. Adam as they strained to drag Monarch onto the tarpaulin.

Finally, with the stag lying on his side on the canvas, they pulled him along the trail to the trailer.

Pulling the sleeping stag up the ramp, Mandy felt as if

her arms were about break. The stag was one of the heaviest animals she'd ever had to lift. *Even heavier than those seal pups*, she thought, remembering the pair of four-month-old harp seals she and a friend, Bart, had found tangled in fishing nets in Goose Bay in Canada. Weak from loss of blood and dehydration, the pups wouldn't have survived without treatment, so Mandy and Bart had hauled them up a ramp of snow onto a sled and dragged them home.

At least we don't have to drag Monarch all the way to the shed, Mandy thought when he was safely inside the trailer. She took her coat off his head. His eyes were closed and he looked quite peaceful. Only the deep gash on his chest and the blood seeping onto the tarpaulin revealed what he'd been through.

It was a very bumpy drive to the forest station. More than once, Mandy feared the jolts would make Monarch wake up and that he'd try to break out. But there was no banging from the trailer and when they finally pulled up in front of the small wooden shed, she breathed a huge sigh of relief.

She jumped out and took a look at the stag's temporary home. It was situated in a glade, about 150 feet away from a log cabin that served as a field office for the park rangers. The shed was about the size of a single garage with a stable door and a small window set high up in the back wall. Some bales of hay were stacked inside, and there was straw strewn on the floor.

"It's like Monarch was expected," Mandy said, noticing that the straw was fresh.

"He *was* expected." Rollo smiled. "I radioed one of my colleagues and asked him to get the place ready."

They hauled the stag out of the trailer and shuffled through the door of the shed. Inside, they carefully rolled him off the tarpaulin onto the clean straw.

While her dad took another look at the wound, Mandy had her first chance to touch the stag. She was amazed at how soft his coat was. "Almost like silk." She touched his antlers. "But these are hard — like bone."

"They are bone," said Rollo. "Not horn, as some think. And believe it or not, he's only been growing them since spring."

"That's amazing!" Mandy said. "He must be very young."

Rollo shook his head. "No, all stags shed their antlers in spring. Replacements start growing immediately. This stag is at least seven because he has a classical head, which is a fancy way of saying his antlers are fully developed."

"What a waste for adult stags to have to get rid of a

full set of antlers and start all over again," Mandy said. She counted the points. "Twelve."

"We call that a 'Royal,'" said Rollo.

"Why?"

"Probably because twelve is the most a Highland stag will achieve," answered Rollo.

"Well, royal's just perfect," Mandy said. "Seeing as his name is Monarch."

Mandy's dad was soaking a ball of cotton wool in antiseptic. He glanced up at Mandy. "He's hardly a monarch, more a young pretender to the throne. One that's been defeated."

"I still think he should be called Monarch," Mandy insisted. "Because he'll have his own herd one day."

"Let's hope so," said Dr. Adam. He cleaned a small area on the stag's front leg before shaving off the fur. When he'd finished, he prepared another syringe. "I'll give him a stronger dose of anesthetic to make sure he's asleep while I stitch him up."

"How long do you think we'll have to keep him here?" Mandy asked, watching her dad insert the needle.

"Not too long," answered Rollo. "We don't want him becoming so used to us that he loses his fear of man. If he's not improving in a few days, we might have to reconsider things."

Mandy didn't want to think what "reconsider things" meant.

When Dr. Adam had finished patching up the injuries, Mandy got a bucket from the trailer and filled it with water from a tap outside the field office. Monarch was bound to be thirsty when he woke up. She put the bucket next to the stag, and Rollo dragged a bale of hay close to him so that he'd have enough food.

"Time to wake him up," said Dr. Adam, and he injected Monarch with an antidote to bring him around. "And time for us to get out of here. We don't want him to see us."

They went outside, closing the door quietly. They peeked through some gaps in the slotted walls until they saw Monarch stir. He looked around, and Mandy thought he seemed puzzled by his surroundings. After a while, his head flopped back onto the ground. *He must be feeling a little groggy,* she thought.

There was nothing more to be done now so they headed home.

"Can we come back in a little while to check on him?" Mandy asked as they drove away.

"He needs some time on his own to settle down," said her dad. "We'll come back this evening to see how he's doing."

Rollo glanced over his shoulder. "Don't you have another urgent mission today, Mandy?"

"Oh! Yeah!" Mandy exclaimed. "The Nelsons must think I'm not coming."

"Don't worry. We'll drop you at Loch Fyne and pick you up later," said Rollo. "And we'll pick up your bike on the way back."

"Thanks," Mandy said. She looked around and caught a last glimpse of the shed before it vanished through the trees. She pictured Monarch lying there all alone. She hoped he wasn't too frightened by his unfamiliar surroundings. *But it's only for a short time. Just until you are well enough to go back to the forest.*

Eight

"It's just a matter of getting her used to flapping things," Mandy explained. She was in the kitchen at Loch Fyne telling the Nelsons her plans to help Jewel. "Starting with small things and building up to full-sized plastic sheets."

"That'll take forever," Zach said gloomily. "She's been scared her whole life. How can we make her change in time for the show?"

"With perseverance," said Mrs. Nelson. "It's a good plan, but don't be disappointed if she isn't ready by the weekend. It might take a lot longer than we hope." She passed around mugs of hot chocolate. "Still, Jewel learns fast. Remember how quickly she was broken in?"

"That was different," argued Faye. "She wasn't frightened of the training."

"No, and given the chance, she can learn not to be afraid of things flapping in the wind," said her mom. "Mandy's idea makes sense. And it's worth trying for Jewel's sake. It can't be fun to be frightened of things all the time."

Faye looked out the window. "It's not."

Mandy finished her cocoa and stood up. "Let's start," she said.

"We should get her into her stable first so that she feels safe," said Faye, reversing her chair away from the table.

"And we can bolt the door to stop her from running away again," said Zach.

Mrs. Nelson frowned. "You'll have to be very careful in the stable. If she gets jittery, she could start jumping around and hurt you."

"We'll be careful," Zach promised. He helped Faye to maneuver through the doorway. "I tell you what, though, if it works, I'll . . . I'll . . ." He looked around, and saw his boots. "I'll eat my boots!"

When Jewel saw Mandy and the others approaching her paddock, she cantered to the railings to greet them.

Mandy reached over the fence to rub her nose. Jewel had clearly been rolling on the ground. Her waterproof New Zealand horse blanket, normally green, had brown muddy patches all over it. There was mud in her tangled mane and tail, and even the tips of her woolly ears were caked in it.

"It looks like you've been having fun," Mandy joked.

"And guess who's going to have clean her up?" said Zach, shaking his head, but smiling at the same time.

"I'll help you," Mandy offered.

Zach opened the gate and led Jewel out. Peanut and Glen were in the same paddock. They trotted over to the railings, too.

"We'll bring you in after Jewel's lesson," Faye promised, reaching up to pat them.

"What's the first step?" asked Zach. "Do you have any ideas, Mandy?"

"Let's think of all the flapping things that have scared her so far," she suggested.

"There was the horse blanket that day she bolted to Mr. Nesbitt's," said Faye.

"And a flag on the back of a motorcycle," Mandy said, remembering.

Faye went ahead to open Jewel's stable. "There were all the banners at the show grounds," she called over her shoulder.

"And the plastic sheet when we were out trail riding," said Zach. He led Jewel into the stable and took off her blanket.

Mandy followed him in. "They all make a lot of noise, or billow out a lot," she said as Zach draped the blanket over the partition wall. "We should start by shaking soft things that don't make any noise."

"Like a blanket," said Faye, who was parked just inside the door. "I'll get one."

While she went back to the house, Mandy and Zach tackled the mud on Jewel's coat. Mandy brushed her body and mane with a soft brush, and Zach untangled her tail with his fingers.

Mandy watched him working gently through the knotted hair. "Wouldn't it be easier to brush her tail?"

"That would split the hairs," Zach explained. "Which wouldn't look good in the show ring."

"Right," Mandy said. She felt a flicker of hope; Zach wouldn't have mentioned the show ring if he didn't believe that they could help Jewel.

Faye returned with a tartan picnic blanket.

"That's perfect," Mandy said, taking it from her. Careful not to make any sudden movements, she draped it over Jewel's back and started rubbing it along her spine and down her sides. The pony stood very still.

"She probably thinks she's being groomed," said Faye.

"I bet she does," Mandy said.

Zach was still untangling the pony's tail. "That means she's not learning anything."

Faye shot him an impatient look. "We can't start with sudden movements that'll spook her. The slower we go, the better, so that she doesn't notice the changes."

"I guess so," said Zach. "But at this rate it will take forever."

"If it does, it does," said his sister firmly.

"Let's try something different," Mandy said. She brought the blanket around in front of Jewel. "It's just a blanket. Nothing to worry about," she said, rubbing the mare's neck. She signaled to Zach to take over. "Keep it next to her. If she stays calm, Faye and I will reward her with the carrots." She took them out of her pocket and gave a few to Faye.

Zach let the blanket slide slowly down Jewel's neck. At the same time he flicked it very slightly.

Jewel didn't react.

"Good pony," Mandy said, offering her a carrot while Zach repeated the exercise.

"This is great," said Faye. "Jewel can see the blanket flapping but she's not scared because it doesn't make a horrible noise. Make it flap a bit more, Zach, so she understands that flapping things won't hurt her."

Zach shook it harder. Jewel lifted her head sharply

and opened her eyes wide for a moment. Mandy held her breath, but the pony settled down and continued crunching up her carrot. When she'd finished it, she sniffed Mandy's pocket for more.

"Just one more," Mandy said, giving it to her. "You've got to work a little harder for the next one." She looked at Zach. "Let's see what she does if we fold it in front of her."

"I'll be ready with the carrots," said Faye, positioning herself close to Jewel.

Mandy and Zach stood in front of the pony. They held the blanket horizontally between them. "We'd better do this very slowly," Mandy said. She remembered Mrs. Nelson telling them to be careful in case Jewel started jumping around. Mandy and Zach could probably get out of her way in time, but it would be harder for Faye.

Jewel wasn't at all upset at the sight of the blanket being folded. She was more interested in the carrot Faye was offering her. She bent her head to take it. "Good girl," said Faye, stroking her nose.

Mandy and Zach unfolded the blanket again. "Let's give it a good shake now," Mandy suggested. They flicked it hard so that it billowed up between them.

Jewel took a step to the side and stared at the blanket suspiciously.

Mandy didn't dare move it again. Zach seemed nervous, too. "Now what?" he whispered.

"We simply continue," said Faye. "Jewel's not going to panic. She's just being cautious." She reached up and patted the pony's shoulder. "Come on, girl. It's only a silly old blanket."

Her soothing tone seemed to win the pony over. Jewel accepted the carrot Faye offered her, ignoring Mandy and Zach while they folded up the blanket.

"That's probably enough for one session," Mandy said. "We shouldn't push our luck."

They were leaving the stable when Dr. Adam and Rollo drove into the yard. "How did it go?" asked Dr. Adam.

"Better than I thought," said Zach. "She didn't get too nervous when we shook a blanket in front of her."

"That sounds hopeful," said Rollo.

"I guess so," Mandy said. "But we've still got a lot of work to do if Jewel's going to be ready for the show."

"Are we going to check on Monarch?" Mandy asked as soon as they were driving away from Loch Fyne. Even though she'd been concentrating on Jewel all afternoon, the stag was never far from her mind.

"Yes, he's next on our list," said Rollo.

At the forest station, they parked some distance from the shed so that the engine wouldn't disturb Monarch and walked the rest of the way. Because it was getting dark, Rollo took a flashlight from the Land Rover.

At the shed, Dr. Adam opened the door just a crack, and Rollo shone the flashlight inside.

Mandy peered in, not sure what to expect. Monarch was curled up on the straw with his head between his front legs. "Poor Monarch," she whispered. It worried her that the bucket of water and the bale of hay seemed untouched.

Dr. Adam put his arm around her. "I know it's hard, but we've done everything we can. It's up to Monarch now."

In the narrow beam of light, Mandy saw Monarch lift his head. Her heart skipped a beat as the stag looked straight at her. She tried to read the expression in his eyes. She was desperate for another glimpse of the proud, wild look she'd seen on his face earlier. She wanted to believe he *was* fighting back and that he would be able to take his place in the wild again.

But his gaze was empty. He looked utterly defeated. *It's like he has no hope of getting better*, Mandy thought with dismay.

Mandy got an early start the next day. Her dad and Rollo and Cara were up early, too. They planned to hike up a nearby mountain — Ben Ime — that morning, after they'd checked on Monarch.

"It would have been good to have you join us," Cara said, giving Mandy a bag of apples from the orchard at Longshadows. "But I know you can't afford to miss a moment working with Jewel."

Mandy swallowed her last spoonful of oatmeal. "I'll check on Monarch on my way to the stable," she said, standing up.

"The shed's not really on your way," said Rollo.

He didn't know her well enough to know that Mandy would have visited the stag even if it meant she had to go in the opposite direction. "It's only a detour," she said.

She put on her coat, which still bore a faint scent of the stag, and hurried out to get her bike. When she arrived at the hut, she gingerly opened the top of the stable door and looked inside.

Monarch was lying exactly as she'd last seen him. The water and hay were untouched.

Mandy bit her lip. *Wild animals are much more sensitive than domestic ones*, she reminded herself. *Monarch still needs to get over the shock.*

She tried to shrug off a feeling of dread that Monarch might not recover. *He's strong and young. That's got to count in his favor.*

She studied him as closely as she could from the door. At least the wound looked clean, and the stitches were holding.

"Don't lose hope," she whispered. "Concentrate on getting better and you'll be back where you belong soon."

The stag blinked at her.

With a heavy heart, Mandy left him and cycled on to Loch Fyne. There, she found Zach nailing a sheet of plastic to the fence beside Jewel's stable. "What's that for?" she asked.

"It'll flap in the wind at night," said Zach, tapping in a nail. "That way, Jewel can get used to flapping noises while she's in her stable."

"Great idea," Mandy said.

Faye was already in the stable with Jewel, feeding her little pieces of apple. "Her favorite," she smiled when Mandy went in.

"That's good," Mandy said, stroking Jewel. "I brought apples, too." She shrugged off her backpack and put it in one corner. "Can we get started?"

"Just a sec," said Zach.

Mandy looked outside. Zach was wrapping the plastic around the rail. "The wind's picked up," he explained. "We don't want this to scare Jewel when she comes out."

Once the plastic was secured, Mandy buckled on Jewel's halter and led her into the yard.

"I thought we should begin where we left off," said Faye. She held up the picnic blanket.

"That's what I was thinking," Mandy said, taking the blanket from Faye.

With Faye sitting at a safe distance in case Jewel acted up, and Zach holding the lead rope, Mandy showed the tartan blanket to Jewel. "Remember this?" She gave it a vigorous shake. Jewel pricked her ears, but didn't move away.

"She doesn't mind it at all," Zach said, sounding pleased.

Just then, a feed bag blew across the yard. Jewel reared up, kicking out her front legs. Zach held on tightly, his face grim as she landed on all fours again, her front hooves clattering on the cobbles.

She's so easily frightened, Mandy thought in dismay.

"I spoke too soon." Zach shook his head. "It's not your fault, I know, girl. But, you sure are a skittish pony!"

"We've just got to keep working with her," Mandy said.

"Look, Mandy," said Zach. "It's really good of you to help us. But let's face it, we'll never be able to trust Jewel in the ring. I don't think there's anything we can do to change that."

Mandy felt as if the breath had been knocked out of her. "But we've only —" she began.

"Zachary Nelson!" Faye sounded so stern, Mandy jumped. "I can't believe you said that." She wheeled herself over to her brother and stopped squarely in front of him. "Aren't you the one who wouldn't let me give up? Who insisted I got back in the saddle as soon as I could sit up straight again? Who persuaded me to stay on Glen's back when all I wanted to do was get into my wheelchair?"

Mandy looked at Zach in surprise. He had obviously understood how important it was for Faye to be able to ride again, yet he must have been terrified for her to get back on a horse after witnessing her terrible accident. But for Faye's sake, he'd pushed that fear aside, and that was why she was able to continue doing what she loved most.

Zach answered his sister softly. "Yes, but you had good reason to be scared."

"And Jewel can't help being afraid, either," said Faye. "It's not her fault. We have to encourage her to be brave, just like you encouraged me."

There was an uncomfortable pause. Mandy took the rope from Zach and led Jewel across the yard. She looked across the paddocks where the other Loch Fyne ponies were grazing peacefully. Beyond them was the dark

green stretch of pine forest. Somewhere in those trees was the tiny log cabin where Monarch was resting. He needed encouragement, too. But how could you do that with an animal you couldn't get close to, let alone touch?

Faye was talking to her brother again. "It's thanks to you, Zach, that my accident didn't stop me from getting back on a horse. But now, at the first little hurdle, you want to give up. That's no way to achieve a dream."

The atmosphere was so tense, Mandy felt it pressing in on her. Faye was right, and of all people, she should know what she was talking about. But Zach had a point, too. Jewel had her own big hurdle to get over. Was there enough time? Mandy hugged the pony. *I want so badly to help you, Jewel.* The little mare snuffled at her hand, planting velvety pony kisses on her palm.

"You know, Faye . . ." Zach said slowly. "You're one incredible sister!"

Mandy looked around. Zach was hugging Faye.

"Jewel *does* deserve a chance," Zach continued. He straightened up and motioned to Mandy. "Let's keep going."

Mandy let out a sigh of relief. She led Jewel back to Zach and Faye. "Should we just continue with the blanket?"

"It's all we can do for now," said Zach.

For half an hour, they flapped the blanket next to Jewel, sometimes quietly and sometimes noisily. When she was calm, they praised her, and Faye offered her pieces of apple.

Gradually, Jewel grew less nervous. Mandy was thrilled when she realized the pony barely noticed the blanket when it made a flapping noise. "It's like she's bored with it now," she said.

"Let's try something else," suggested Zach. "There's an old New Zealand blanket in the tack room." He sprinted across the yard to get it.

Faye and Mandy had just enough time to exchange a cheerful look and for Faye to say quietly, "He's a lot more positive now," before Zach returned with the green canvas blanket.

They showed it to Jewel before Zach started to shake it. Mandy was delighted when Jewel ignored it.

Zach looked surprised and relieved. "I misjudged her," he said after a while. He held the canvas in both hands and flipped it hard. It flew up with a loud crack.

It was like an electric current shot through Jewel. She reared up, jerking the lead rope so hard that she nearly broke free.

"Whoa!" Mandy said, struggling to hold on to the rope.

Zach dropped the blanket and grabbed Jewel's halter. "That was a close one," he puffed.

Mandy thought he looked disappointed again.

"She needs to be a lot better than that if she's going to go into the ring," said Zach and letting go of her, he ran back to the house.

So that's it, Mandy thought gloomily. *He's given up.*

"So much for my pep talk." Faye sighed. She wheeled herself over to Mandy. "And you were doing so well, Jewel." The pony dropped her head so that Faye could reach up and rub her nose.

"I guess we were being a little too ambitious with this," Mandy said. She bent down to pick up the New Zealand blanket.

"Let's forget that for now!" a voice from behind them said.

"Zach?" Faye spun her chair around.

Mandy saw Zach hurrying back across the yard. He was carrying a pile of brightly colored cloths. "Pillowcases!" He grinned. "I snuck them from the linen closet. They're exactly what we need."

"They are?" Faye sounded doubtful.

"Uh-huh. I think we should start again with things that flap but don't make a big noise," said Zach. "Here . . ." He gave Faye one end of a length of nylon rope and Mandy a box of pegs. "We'll peg the pillow-cases to this line and hang it along the paddock fence, and across the gate. That way, Jewel can see flapping things all the time, not just when we're shaking them next to her. After a while, we can start bringing in some more serious things."

"Great idea," Mandy said. "The pillowcases will look like streamers, just like at the show ground."

"Exactly," said Zach.

When the rainbow-colored streamers were ready, Zach let Jewel sniff them before he went to decorate the paddock. From where she and Faye were waiting with the mare, Mandy watched the pillowcases waving in the breeze. It really did remind her of a show ring.

Zach sprinted back. "Time to go into your paddock, Jewel."

Mandy and Zach led her across. Faye wheeled herself next to them, the bag of apples ready on her lap. For most of the way, Jewel walked along calmly. But she shied away when they approached the streamers.

"Steady, girl," said Zach. He gripped her lead rope with both hands.

Mandy stroked Jewel. "You've seen worse than that."

Jewel didn't seem to agree. She pulled at the rope while staring suspiciously at the pillowcases.

"I'll try to get her to follow me in," said Faye. She went ahead and parked herself behind the fence. "Come on, Jewel. I've got a whole bag of apples for you."

Jewel refused to budge. Zach tugged the lead rope. "Let's go."

"We're putting too much pressure on her," Mandy said, worried they'd make things worse.

Suddenly, the pony jerked her head and reared up. This time, the lead rope flew out of Zach's hands.

"Hey!" he yelled. Jewel charged forward, nearly knocking him over.

Still clinging to the halter, Mandy felt herself being almost dragged along. "Whoa!" she cried as she and the pony hurtled past the streamers and into the paddock.

Stumbling along at the pony's side, Mandy finally lost her grip on the halter. She let go and came to an abrupt stop just inside the paddock. Jewel galloped on, stopping when she was halfway across the field. She whirled around and stood stiff-legged, snorting.

Zach ran up to Mandy. "That was a big surprise!"

"At least she went past the streamers," Mandy said.

"Yeah. At least," muttered Zach.

They went over to Jewel and Zach unclipped the lead rope. The pony cantered away, flicking up her heels.

Oh well, thought Mandy, watching her. *There's still a long way to go. But it's a start.*

Nine

Mandy watched as Mrs. Nelson stuck the knife into the top of the turnip and chipped out a tiny segment. It looked like trying to hollow out a rock!

"Are you planning on finishing that before Halloween?" she joked.

Mrs. Nelson smiled. "It's not an easy job, that's for sure. But you know how to go a long way, don't you?"

"How?"

"One step at a time." Mrs. Nelson switched the machine on.

Mandy nodded. "I guess two steps at a time would be impossible." She thought about the work they'd done with Jewel so far. They *had* been going step-by-step, sometimes going back a step. But they had at least moved forward with the streamers episode.

The next step would be to introduce some noisier billowing objects, but they were giving Jewel a few hours' break. They were using the time to start preparing for the Halloween party.

Zach looked up from where he was sketching designs for a turnip face on a sheet of plain paper. The plan was for Mandy, Zach, and Faye to decide what the turnips should look like while Mrs. Nelson did the tricky job of carving. Zach frowned as his mother extracted another sliver of turnip. "At this rate, we'll be lucky to have one turnip for the party," he said. "We should have bought some of Mr. Nesbitt's pumpkins instead."

"Well, you were the one who wanted me to experience some real Scottish traditions," Mandy reminded him.

Zach made a face. "I should have left this one out. There are plenty of others. Like dooking fur aiples."

"Like *what*?" It sounded like Zach was speaking in a foreign language!

"It's the Scottish version of apple bobbing," Mrs. Nelson explained. "He's actually saying 'ducking for apples.'"

"I think we should just cover ourselves in turnip

chunks and go out trick-or-treating," Mandy said, brushing some pieces of turnip off the table.

There was a knock at the front door. "I'll get it," said Zach. He went out and returned with Mr. Nesbitt.

"Good news!" Zach exclaimed. "The turnips are history. We've got pumpkins instead. Thanks to you, Mandy."

"Me?"

"Yes," said the farmer. "It's my way of thanking you for leading the pony out of my pumpkin crop."

"I'm glad I did," Mandy said. If she hadn't, she'd never have got involved with Jewel, nor would she have made such great new friends.

They got the pumpkins from Mr. Nesbitt's van. They were gigantic!

"I thought you deserved the best of the crop," said the farmer, carefully putting one on Faye's lap. "Not too heavy, is it?" he said, checking.

Faye shook her head.

"They'll be a lot easier to carve than those little turnips!" continued Mr. Nesbitt, following them into the kitchen and setting the last pumpkin down on the table.

"That's for sure," said Mrs. Nelson.

Mandy and Zach cleared away the turnips while Mrs. Nelson and Mr. Nesbitt set to work on the pumpkins, carefully carving the designs from the sheets of paper.

Before long, three hollowed-out jack-o'-lanterns sat on the table.

Mandy looked at each one. "Your's looks the friendliest," she said to Faye. The pumpkin had a neat, smiling face. "But Zach's looks like a ghoul!" It had a toothy grin and very large nose.

"It's not *that* bad." Zach laughed.

"It's worse," teased Faye. "It's the ugliest jack-o'-lantern I've ever seen."

"And Mandy's is the strangest one," countered Zach.

Mandy had to agree. Mr. Nesbitt had done a great job of copying her intricate design of horseshoes circling all the way around the pumpkin. "Call it a new Scottish tradition." She grinned.

With the pumpkin carving complete, they returned to Jewel for her afternoon session.

"How about that?" Mandy exclaimed when the pony trotted straight over to the gate to meet them, giving Zach's streamers only the briefest glance.

Faye gave the pony a piece of apple. "You're a clever girl, Jewel."

"The other ponies could have helped," Mandy suggested. Peanut and Glen hadn't even blinked at the string of pillowcases. Their confidence might have rubbed off on Jewel.

"Whatever it is, it's definitely working," said Zach.

They spent another half hour shaking a bedsheet and some giant bath towels close to Jewel. When she came to the paddock to check on how things were going, Mrs. Nelson's eyes widened at the sight of her linens being waved and tossed around. "At least it can be washed," she said with a resigned sigh. She shot a wistful glance at a grubby white towel lying on the ground.

After Mrs. Nelson had gone back to the house, Mandy suggested stepping up the challenges. "Let's hold a sheet against the wind so that it blows out," she said.

"OK, but not too close to Jewel at first," said Zach.

Faye stayed near the pony to distract her with apples

while Mandy and Zach took the sheet to the other side of the paddock. They each held one end of it so that it strained against the wind.

Mandy saw Jewel glance across at it. "She doesn't look too worried, does she?"

"Let's see what happens if we go closer," said Zach.

Jewel was calm until a gust of wind made the sheet snap loudly. She galloped away, snorting.

"Too soon!" Faye called out.

They tried the same exercise again, keeping well away from Jewel. Most of the time she ignored the sheet, but when it surged out and cracked in the wind, she galloped across the paddock.

"Let's call it a day," Zach said eventually. "She deserves some peace now."

They folded up the linens and towels and took them back to the house.

"I suppose she is slightly better," said Faye. "I mean, she doesn't mind billowing things as much as she used to."

Zach opened the back door and stood aside for Faye to go through. "That's true. But she still can't stand the noise."

"We've really got to work on that," Mandy said. She tried to ignore a sneaking feeling that Jewel's fear was so deep-rooted, it was going to take a lot longer to deal with than she had thought.

They put the linens and towels on a chair in the kitchen, ready for the next day's training. Faye made them all some hot chocolate and they drank it while discussing the next step.

"I suppose we just keep on going," said Zach.

"It's all we can do," Mandy agreed.

"We're going to be really busy tomorrow," Faye reminded them. There were still the Halloween preparations to finish in between the sessions with Jewel.

"I'll get here as early as I can," Mandy promised.

Riding away from Loch Fyne ten minutes later, Mandy started thinking about Monarch again. Had he started eating and drinking yet? Was he on his feet? Would he be trying to find a way out of the shed?

Dusk was settling by the time she reached the shed. She opened the top of the door just a crack so that she could look in without disturbing Monarch.

He was lying in exactly the same position as when Mandy saw him last. *He hasn't moved!* She could have wept with disappointment. She stared at him and went ice-cold. *He's not breathing!* Panic gripped her, but then, in the fading light, she saw his rib cage expand as he drew in a breath.

Mandy closed her eyes with relief.

When she opened them, Monarch was looking straight at her. "We're trying to help you," she told him quietly. "But you need to eat to get strong again."

Monarch blinked, breaking eye contact. He turned his head and started pulling at the hay in front of him.

Mandy stared in astonishment. *He understood what I was saying!*

Munching a mouthful of straw, Monarch looked at her again. The blank expression Mandy had seen in his eyes was gone. Now, there was a glimmer of something else. Wariness, perhaps? *It could even be determination*, Mandy thought.

Whatever it was, something had changed in Monarch. To Mandy, it was a sign that he hadn't given up.

The following day was Halloween, the last day in October. Mandy arrived at Loch Fyne in time to help take Jewel, Glen, and Peanut to the paddock. It was a cold, blustery morning, with heavy black clouds scooting across the sky.

"Perfect weather for working with Jewel," Mandy said, feeling the wind tug at her hair.

They opened the gate to the paddock and unclipped the ponies' lead ropes. Jewel trotted straight past the streamers as if they weren't there.

"Excellent!" Mandy said, feeling very hopeful.

Zach got the linens they'd used the day before. They started by quietly shaking the towels and blanket, moving on to folding and unfolding a big sheet and flicking the towels. Jewel flinched and rolled her eyes at the snapping noise, but didn't run off. And when Faye offered her an apple, she calmed down completely

"She's looking good," Mandy said after a while.

"She was looking good yesterday, too," Zach pointed out, "until we started making the really big noises."

Faye bent down to pick up the sheet. "We're just going in circles doing the same safe things. We have to take a few risks to see if we're making real progress."

"Right. It's the billowing-sheet treatment," said Zach.

Mandy took the bedsheet from Faye. Yesterday it had been spotless and white. Today, it looked as if it had been used to wipe floors.

While Faye distracted Jewel with pieces of apple, Mandy and Zach held the sheet between them. The wind pulled at it, making it sway back and forth over the grass.

Jewel ignored it.

"We've got to let it flap around," Zach told Mandy. "Let's hold it higher."

They lifted their arms so that the sheet was well above the ground. Suddenly, it flew up, cracking like thunder.

Jewel bolted.

"Oh, no!" Mandy groaned.

"Let's give her a break and go in for lunch," said Faye. "We need to finish the Halloween preparations, too."

"OK. But let's tie the sheet to a tree," said Zach. "If it flaps around long enough, Jewel's *got* to get used to it."

"Like the pillowcases," said Faye.

"Except they didn't sound like thunder," Mandy reminded her.

There was a pine tree just outside the paddock. Zach climbed onto the fence and tied the sheet to a branch. It hung limply for a few seconds until a fresh gust of wind picked it up. The sheet bulged out, straining to break loose from the branch. The wind tugged at it, making it surge and sink and swell out again.

Mandy looked at the pony on the far side of the paddock. Jewel had her back to the sheet, but she kept glancing around nervously. Mandy wondered if it was fair to make Jewel put up with it.

"I hope she can handle it," said Faye. Like Mandy, she must have been seeing the flapping sheet through the pony's eyes.

Zach jumped down from the fence. "Let's watch her for a while. If she gets really spooked, we'll take it down."

They waited for ten minutes. Jewel stayed on the far side of the paddock, looking up from time to time.

"She's not exactly happy, but she's not panicking," said Zach. "I think we can leave her for a while."

They went back to the house where they found Mrs. Nelson peeling potatoes in the kitchen.

"Are those for *champit tatties*?" Zach asked.

Mrs. Nelson nodded.

Champit tatties! Mandy wondered what kind of dish that was.

"It's another Scottish Halloween tradition," Faye said, slicing a loaf of bread. "We hide things like thimbles and wishbones in a bowl of mashed potatoes. Everyone takes a spoonful and depending on what you get, you'll know what the future holds for you."

"Oh, I'm sure!" Mandy chuckled, buttering the slices of bread. Fortune-telling mashed potatoes? James was going to love hearing about that!

"It works," Zach said seriously. "Last year, I got the thimble. It meant I wouldn't get married." He grinned. "And I haven't."

Mandy and Faye laughed. Mrs. Nelson put the potatoes in a saucepan. "Well, the Halloween year's not quite done yet," she said. "Your wife could show up on the doorstep any minute."

"I'd run a mile," Zach promised, smearing peanut butter onto a piece of bread.

After lunch, they got some apples from the shed and put them in a plastic tub, ready for the apple-bobbing game. All the time, Mandy was itching to go back to the paddock. When they did, Mandy kept her fingers crossed. "I hope Jewel's ignoring the noisy sheet," she said. "And that she's gotten closer to it."

Her heart sank when she saw the pony still standing as far away from it as possible. Every time the sheet cracked, Jewel flinched.

"It's not working," Zach said gloomily.

"Maybe she needs a longer break," said Faye. "We can't expect her to put up with things she's scared of all day, every day."

Mandy leaned over the fence. "You mean take down the streamers and the sheet?"

"No. Let's give her a change of scene and go out for another trail ride," said Faye. "We'll be OK if we keep away from the main road."

"Good idea," Mandy said. Seeing the lovely pony looking so miserable, Mandy was starting to wonder if they were making a big mistake. Instead of helping Jewel deal with flapping things, they could be making things worse for her. *Just like helping Monarch could stress him out*, she thought.

"A trail ride would be good, but it's too late now," Zach said. "It'll be dark in an hour. And we still haven't finished everything for the party. Let's just get the ponies in and we'll go out in the morning."

They took the ponies back to the stables where they rubbed them down and gave them their feed.

Mandy hugged Jewel before she left the stable. "We're going to have some fun tomorrow. No nasty flapping things, just a lovely ride through the forest."

The pony nuzzled Mandy's hair. Outside, the plastic sheet flapped and snapped in the breeze. "Sorry you have to put up with that all night," Mandy said.

But the pony didn't seem too troubled by it. She was more interested in the apple Mandy had saved for her. The plastic wasn't as noisy as the cracking sheet, and Jewel couldn't see it billowing out. *Or perhaps she's gotten used to it*, Mandy thought. Although she was a bit down about the way things had gone that afternoon, she hadn't given up hope yet.

It was almost completely dark when Mandy and the twins went back to the house. The wind had picked up. Trees groaned dramatically, and Mandy pulled her jacket more tightly around her. She looked up and saw the clouds drift apart. The moon, full and bright, looked back down at her. Black shapes, like wide upside-down *W*'s, emerged from the shadows. Bats! They darted in the silvery moonlight, silhouetted against the bright white jack-o'-lantern in the sky.

It was a perfect night for Halloween.

Mandy and the twins had just finished stirring the objects into the mashed potatoes when a car pulled up outside. "That must be Dad and Rollo and Cara," Mandy said. Mrs. Nelson had invited them to the party, too.

Mandy ran outside to meet them — mainly to find out how Monarch was doing. "Is he still eating? Has he stood up yet? Is he looking stronger?"

"Yes, no, and perhaps," answered her dad, opening his door.

Good news and not so good news. But at least it wasn't bad.

Dr. Adam climbed out of the Land Rover and squeezed Mandy's shoulders. "I know you were hoping for better news, sweetie. But Monarch's in the best place right now. Try to put him out of your mind for a few hours and enjoy the fun."

The party took place in the Nelsons' huge living room. With its high ceilings and exposed beams it was the ideal Halloween setting. An log fire crackled and popped in the hearth.

"The fire's not just for warmth," said Mrs. Nelson,

tossing a log onto the grate. "Centuries ago, the Druids lit fires at Halloween to ward off evil." She dimmed the lights so that the flames cast eery shadows on the walls.

"Between those shadows and that ghoulish pumpkin . . ." Dr. Adam pointed to Zach's jack-o'-lantern on the mantel, ". . . you'd think we were *inviting* evil rather than keeping it away!"

The party started off with everyone bobbing for apples. The idea was to catch an apple, peel it in a single strip, and toss it over your shoulder.

"The shape when it lands is the initial of your future husband or wife," explained Faye.

When Mandy threw her apple strip, it landed in the shape of an *S*.

"Aha!" grinned Dr. Adam said, grinning. "Seamus."

"Seamus!" Mandy frowned. "I don't know anyone with that name."

"Oh, but you do," said her dad. "It's the Irish version of James."

Mandy felt herself blush. "James is just a friend," she muttered.

For *champit tatties*, they gathered around the coffee table and dipped their spoons into the mashed potatoes. Zach was the first to find something. It was a coin.

"You're going to be rich." Mrs. Nelson laughed. "I hope you remember your family!"

Mandy dipped her spoon in. "A wishbone."

"Lucky you," Mrs. Nelson said, smiling. "That means your biggest wish will be granted."

"Pull it with me," Mandy said, holding it out to Faye.

As it snapped in two, Mandy met Faye's eyes. They smiled at each other as they made their secret wishes. But Mandy was sure she knew what Faye had wished for. *The same as me. That Jewel would beat her fear.*

And just in case there was anything in the old traditions, Mandy made another wish. *Let Monarch get better, too.*

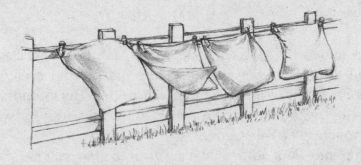

Ten

"He's standing!" Mandy whispered as she peeped through the wooden slats of the shed.

Monarch was on his feet, munching the pile of hay!

It was early the next morning, and Mandy was at the shed with her dad and Rollo.

A shaft of soft autumn sunlight pierced the window in the back wall. It bathed Monarch in a golden glow and gave his coat a burnished look. Mandy remembered how velvety his fur had felt and she longed to stroke him again.

She knew though there was no chance of that. Monarch was more on edge today than yesterday. He glanced around as if he sensed danger, and Mandy felt her heart quicken. The stag was behaving like a wild creature again, ready to flee at a moment's notice. His temporary refuge was more like a prison now. But was he well enough to be released?

Mandy kept still, not daring even to glance at her dad. A slight movement, a word spoken too loudly, even a scent carried on the wind, could cause Monarch to panic.

"He's very alert," Dr. Adam confirmed in a whisper. "And the wound looks a lot better. He's definitely healing."

At last! "It's what I wished for last night," Mandy admitted. "When can we let him go?"

"Later today?" Rollo checked with Dr. Adam.

Mandy was surprised. "So soon? But he's only just gotten back on his feet."

"He's not likely to challenge other stags until he feels completely better," Rollo explained quietly. "What he needs now is the familiarity of the forest. We'll check on him again after lunch and decide for sure."

Did you hear that, Monarch? Mandy asked silently. *You might be going home!*

When Mandy arrived at the Loch Fyne stable half an hour later, Jewel was looking over her stall door. She whinnied when she saw Mandy.

"Good morning, Jewel." Mandy smiled, going straight

to her. She glanced at the plastic sheeting. It wasn't flapping at all this morning because it was wrapped tightly around the fence rail. The wind in the night must have done that. "We're going to have a wonderful ride today," Mandy said, putting her arms around the pony's neck and kissing her cheek.

Jewel sniffed at her pockets, looking for a tidbit. "You're in luck," Mandy said, grinning and taking out the carrot she'd brought with her.

Zach had already planned their route. "We'll follow the main road for a short way, then we'll go cross-country to a lane that will take us through the forest to the River Gail and on to Loch Goil."

"Sounds great," Mandy said.

They saddled Jewel, Glen, and Peanut and rode out of the yard. When they passed the paddock where the pillowcases fluttered in the breeze, Jewel didn't even react. It was a good start!

"Between you and Monarch, things are looking up," Mandy said, patting Jewel's neck.

"Monarch's doing OK?" said Faye.

"Yes. We might be able to let him go this afternoon," Mandy reported happily.

Faye smiled. "That's terrific."

Zach was trotting a few paces ahead. He slowed Peanut down and said to Mandy, "It'll take a load off your shoulders if the stag can be let free. Except for the party last night, you've been helping animals ever since you got to Scotland."

"No, I haven't." Mandy chuckled. "It's since I was born! But that's the way I like it."

They came to the road and headed east in single file, keeping close to the side of the road. Mandy saw a small carved pumpkin on the wall outside a stone cottage, a reminder of last night's Halloween festivities.

It also reminded Mandy of the first time she'd seen Jewel, knee-deep in pumpkin vines. Who'd have thought she'd ever find a pony in a pumpkin patch?

They rode on, into a light wind that made the trees sway and dead leaves swirl across the ground. Mandy was encouraged when Jewel ignored the brittle leaves. But even they didn't make as much noise as a flapping sheet.

Faye was riding in front now. "That's where we cut across the fields," she said, pointing. A path led away from the road through a field as flat as a tabletop. *Perfect for a canter*, Mandy thought.

They had nearly reached the path when a truck appeared on the road ahead. It started downhill and just as it drew level with the riders, a piece of black plastic flew off the back.

With a deafening flap, the sheet lifted into the air like

a giant bird. Mandy felt Jewel flinch. She tightened her grip on the reins as the sheeting blew across the road straight toward the ponies.

"It's all right, Jewel," Mandy said as calmly as she could. She kept her legs against Jewel's sides, hoping to let her know that everything was OK and she didn't need to be scared. Beside her, she could see Zach doing the same for Peanut. Both ponies lifted their heads in alarm, but stood their ground. Then, to Mandy's horror, Glen reared up.

"Easy!" cried Faye, clinging to the front of her saddle as Glen's hooves crashed to the ground.

Mandy saw Glen start to rear again. She kicked Jewel forward, stretching across to grab Glen's bridle before she could rear up again.

"Steady, girl," Mandy said, feeling Glen struggling to pull away from her. She held the reins tightly and urged Jewel closer to Glen's side so that the ponies were touching each other.

In front of them, the plastic fell to the ground, where it lay like a crumpled wing, looking quiet and non-threatening.

Mandy brought both horses to a halt just as Zach reached them. He steered Peanut to Glen's other side so that she was cocooned between the others. "Are you all right, Faye?" he asked, gasping.

Faye looked flushed and she was breathing hard. But she was smiling!

"I'm fine," Faye said, "thanks to Mandy." She leaned across and patted Jewel's neck. "And to you, too."

"Two near freak accidents in just a few days," said Zach. "So much for trying to school our ponies!"

"Don't you see? This is the best thing that could have happened!" Faye exclaimed.

Mandy frowned. "It is?" Suddenly, she understood what Faye was getting at.

Jewel had just passed her biggest test yet! She'd hardly reacted at all when the plastic sheet flapped toward them, and when Mandy asked her to go forward to help Glen, she hadn't hesitated even when her hooves touched the plastic.

"The plastic next to the stable must have flapped and blown around for hours last night until Jewel got used to the noise and realized it wasn't going to hurt her," Mandy said, thinking aloud. Their plan had worked! "You're cured, Jewel," she said, bending forward and hugging her. "And you're a hero!"

"She's *much* better, Mom," Zach told Mrs. Nelson back at Loch Fyne.

"She was totally calm when that plastic blew off the truck," Mandy put in.

"She practically had to jump over it when Mandy rode her forward to help me and Glen," said Faye.

Mrs. Nelson was sitting on the couch in the living room. Mandy and the twins were crowded eagerly around her.

"Can we enter her in the show?" Zach prompted.

Mrs. Nelson frowned. "You don't think it's a little soon?"

Zach flopped down on the couch next to her. "She was a completely different pony today."

Faye pushed her chair closer to the couch. "And it's all thanks to Mandy."

"Me?" Mandy frowned. As far as she was concerned, they'd all done their part equally.

"The whole plan was your idea in the first place," Faye reminded her. "And you never lost faith that Jewel would get better."

"I wasn't always confident," Mandy admitted.

Mrs. Nelson stood up and went to the phone.

Zach followed her. "So, what about it?" he persisted. "Are we going to enter Jewel?"

Mrs. Nelson picked up the receiver. "I think . . ." She paused while she dialed a number. ". . . that we should give her another chance. I'm going to enter her right now!"

*   *   *

Once Jewel's place in the class had been confirmed, Mandy returned to Longshadows where she told her dad and the McCruishes about the eventful morning.

"It's an amazing story," said Cara.

"Now all we need is Monarch to be well," Mandy said.

"That's what we're going to find out now," said Rollo. "We've been waiting for you to come home so that we can go and take a look at him."

In case they decided to release him, they hitched up the trailer and drove to the forest station. Instead of parking some distance from the shed, Rollo drove right up to it. There would be no sedative and no dragging the stag onto a tarpaulin this time. He'd have to walk into the trailer himself.

They opened the top of the door and looked inside.

Monarch was lying on the straw. Mandy's heart dropped. But when the stag saw them he was on his feet in a flash, scrambling up on his slender legs. He stared at them, his eyes wide.

"He's panicking!" Mandy gasped when Monarch skittered to the back of the shed.

"Good!" Dr. Adam said, which surprised Mandy. "I mean it," her dad continued. "He's moving well and he went into flight mode when he saw us. That means we have a thoroughly wild stag who's really healing."

"Ready to be released, stitches and all?" asked Cara.

"That's right," said Dr. Adam. "And don't worry about the stitches. I used special thread for them. They'll dissolve in time."

The next step was to get Monarch to go into the trailer. Mandy thought it would be a bit like loading a horse, but with one difference. Horses were trained to go in. A stag wasn't.

"We've got to do this efficiently," said Rollo after he'd backed the trailer tight up against the shed door. "We can't have him thrashing around and hurting himself again."

Working silently, Dr. Adam and Rollo opened the shed door and lowered the trailer ramp. Then they clambered out and waited at the side of the shed with Mandy and Cara.

It was five minutes before Monarch finally emerged. He must have realized there was no where to go but forward. At the foot of the ramp, he hesitated, his eyes rolling.

Go into the trailer, Monarch, Mandy begged silently.

Tentatively, the stag took a step forward. He sniffed the air, took another step, paused, then slowly walked up the ramp. As soon as he was in the trailer, Dr. Adam and Rollo ran forward and lifted the ramp, and Mandy and Cara slid the bolts across.

Monarch was inside! But he was also terrified. Mandy

could hear him pacing back and forth inside. A loud bang told her he'd slammed against the side, trying to find a way out.

"Quick, let's go!" said Rollo.

Mandy ran forward to the Land Rover, pausing as she passed the trailer. "Don't be afraid, Monarch," she whispered through the ventilation holes in the side. "You're going home." She would have loved to give him the remains of the carrots in her pocket but she knew Monarch could not be treated like a domestic animal. He was as wild and as free as the golden eagle Mandy had seen the other day.

They drove through the forest for about fifteen minutes before Rollo stopped the Land Rover near where Mandy had found the stag.

"What if he meets the old stag again?" Mandy asked.

Rollo got out and went around to the trailer. "I doubt he'll challenge him again for a while," he said, sliding back the bolts. "And it's better for Monarch to be in familiar territory while he gets his strength back, rather than having to find his way around a new area."

Dr. Adam and Rollo let down the ramp and waited a few yards away with Mandy and Cara.

Monarch stood at the far end of the trailer, not moving.

"Come on," Mandy whispered. "You can go now."

"You'd think he'd make a run for it," Cara murmured.

"I think we should hide," said Mandy. "Then he'll know he's not in danger if he comes out."

"Good idea," said Rollo. "Let's hunch down inside the Land Rover."

It seemed to be exactly what Monarch was waiting for. As soon as they were out of sight, just peeking over the tops of their seats, the stag walked slowly down the ramp. At the bottom, he paused to sniff the air and look around before limping away.

It wasn't quite the dramatic and emotional occasion Mandy had imagined it would be. Nevertheless, even though he walked unevenly, the stag held his head high as he stepped into the trees.

With his regal crown of antlers, he looked as proud as his namesake, Monarch of the Glen.

Eleven

Mandy felt someone shaking her shoulder.

"Wake up, Mandy! It's time to go."

Mandy forced her eyes open. Cara was standing next to her bed.

Mandy rubbed her eyes. "Time to go where?" Suddenly, she remembered. "It's Sunday!" she squeaked, throwing off the bedspread. She looked at her watch. She was due to be at Loch Fyne in less than an hour!

In five minutes she was downstairs where her dad was waiting to give her a lift to the stable.

Nearing Loch Fyne a short while later, Mandy spotted red deer on a hillside. She looked at them through the binoculars. There were eight does and, as usual, a single stag. His "killer" antlers allowed Mandy to identify him at once. "It's Monarch's rival. I'm glad he wasn't hurt," Mandy said. "But he'd better watch out next year. Monarch might not be so easy to beat again."

Dr. Adam dropped Mandy off at Loch Fyne. "See you at the show," he said. He and Rollo and Cara would be joining Mandy and the Nelsons later that morning.

Mandy found everyone was almost ready to leave. Faye was holding Jewel's lead rope while Zach lowered the trailer ramp, and Mrs. Nelson was hurrying over from the tack room with a clean traveling blanket.

"Sorry I'm late," Mandy said, helping Mrs. Nelson drape the blanket over Jewel.

The pony looked as gorgeous as ever this morning. Her jet-black coat gleamed in the sunshine, and her flowing mane fell softly over her shoulders like a silken waterfall. She seemed pleased to see Mandy, nuzzling her neck when Mandy patted her.

"You're not late. We're leaving in a few minutes." Faye smiled. She passed the lead-rope reins to Zach who loaded Jewel into the trailer. Mandy thought he looked tense.

"Jewel's going to be fine," Mandy said as she watched him tie the lead rope to the metal ring at the front of the trailer.

"We haven't tested her with flapping things in crowded places," he said, coming down the ramp. "What if crowds are part of the problem?"

"There were no crowds when she nearly ran into that car the other day," said his sister while Mrs. Nelson helped her into the Land Rover. "Or when she got spooked in the yard and ran to Mr. Nesbitt's farm."

Zach wheeled the chair around to the trailer. "I guess," he said uncertainly.

"It's just stage fright," Faye whispered out her window to Mandy while Zach pushed the wheelchair up the ramp. Out loud, she added, "Things are looking up, remember."

Mandy knew she was referring to Monarch. After the stag had been released, Mandy had phoned the Nelsons with the news. Faye was thrilled, saying it was a good omen for the show.

The show was at Dunoon again. The show ground was even more crowded than before, and the parking lot was jam-packed with vehicles and trailers.

"It's really busy here today," Mandy commented as she helped Faye into her chair.

"Yes, it's a major show," said Faye, "because it's the last chance to qualify for the championships."

While Mrs. Nelson got Zach's number from the

registration tent, Mandy helped to get Jewel ready. She led the pony out of the trailer and tied her to a ring at the side while Zach brought out the saddle.

Faye started to groom Jewel. "See that pony?" She nodded toward a beautiful dapple gray Highland gelding being led out of a trailer nearby. "That's Sea Cottage. He's the one to beat this time."

"He's lovely," agreed Mandy. "But he's not as gorgeous as Jewel."

Zach passed the saddle to Mandy. "Take this for me, please. I'd better put the ramp up so it doesn't take up so much room." Faye had only just managed to squeeze through between the ramp and the truck parked behind it.

Mandy carried the saddle over to Jewel. She was about to put it on the pony's back when Zach let out a yell.

"Ouch!"

"Now what?" said Faye.

Mandy put the saddle on the ground and ran around to see what the problem was. Faye followed, somehow managing to turn her chair in the tight gap.

Zach was bent double, trying to heave the ramp off his foot. Mandy rushed over and lifted the ramp so that he could pull his foot free.

Zach tried to put his foot down but winced and picked

it off the ground right away. "I think it's broken," he groaned.

"Broken!" Faye gasped, staring at her brother as he hopped to the trailer and leaned against it. "I'll get a doctor from the first-aid tent," she said and set off through the parked vehicles.

"I'll come with you," Mandy called. Faye might need help getting through the parking lot.

"No. Stay with Zach," Faye shouted over her shoulder. "I'll be OK." She wheeled herself past a van and disappeared.

Mandy looked at Zach. "You'd better sit down," she said. "You should take your boot off in case your foot is swelling up."

There were a couple of folding stools in the back of the Land Rover. Mandy took one out and opened it for Zach. Leaning on Mandy's arm, he lowered himself onto it and bent forward to remove his boot. He gave it a tug and stopped immediately. "I don't think I can do this," he said, gritting his teeth. "It really hurts."

"Let me try," Mandy offered. She knelt in front of him and rested his foot on her lap. Very slowly, she eased the boot off. Although she was as gentle as possible, she knew it was hurting Zach. He sucked in his breath and squeezed his eyes shut.

When at last the boot was off, he breathed out with relief. "Thanks, Mandy."

"You're number thirteen, Zach." It was Mrs. Nelson, appearing from behind the trailer.

"Thirteen! Go figure," said Zach with a bitter laugh.

"Is Jewel ready?" Mrs. Nelson asked. Then she noticed Zach's foot — even in the sock, it looked very swollen. "Oh, my goodness!" she exclaimed, hurrying over. "What happened?"

"I dropped the ramp on it," said Zach just as Faye returned. A young, dark-haired woman was pushing the chair, and there was a black doctor's bag on Faye's lap.

"This is Dr. Andrews," said Faye.

The doctor crouched in front of Zach and peeled off his sock to examine his foot. It was already bruising and very puffy. She pressed it lightly and asked him to move it from side to side and up and down. "Wiggle your toes if you can," she added.

"It really hurts," he said.

"I'm sure it does," said Dr. Andrews. "But the good news is that it's not broken, just badly bruised."

Mandy and Faye looked at each other and sighed with relief.

"The bad news," the doctor continued, "is that you won't be able to ride for at least week."

Zach's face dropped. "But the show . . ."

The doctor shook her head. "I'm sorry, Zach. Your foot won't be strong enough to support your weight in the stirrup."

Zach swallowed hard and stared at the ground.

Faye put an arm across his back. "It's such bad luck."

"All that hard work for nothing," Zach groaned.

Mandy wanted to tell him that it hadn't been for nothing, that Jewel was a confident, happy pony now, which was what mattered most. But Mrs. Nelson beat her to it.

"Even if we hadn't entered Jewel in the show it would have been worthwhile," she said. "So it's not the end of the world."

"It's definitely not," put in Faye. "Especially since . . ." She smiled at Mandy. ". . . Jewel can still compete in her class."

Zach looked up. "But you heard what Dr. Andrews said."

"You can't ride," said Faye, "but Mandy can."

"Me?" Mandy gulped. "You want me to ride Jewel in the show?"

"Of course! You're absolutely the right person for it," said Mrs. Nelson. She put her hands on Faye's shoulders. "Good thinking, Faye. I'm sure the show registry will allow it if I explain right away." She looked at Mandy. "You do want to ride in Zach's place, don't you?"

Want to! Mandy beamed. "I'd *love* to."

"Then let's get a move on!" Faye said briskly. "You've got to change — Zach's show outfit should fit you — and we still have to tack Jewel up."

For the next ten minutes, Mandy felt as if she were in a whirlwind. She climbed into the trailer to change and was relieved that Zach's outfit fit her quite well even though she had to roll over the waistband of the jodhpurs. When she came out again, feeling very professional in the navy jacket, she found Jewel saddled up.

She pulled on Zach's riding boots then mounted Jewel. It was only when she looked around that she started to feel nervous. Other riders were making their way toward the ring. They looked very experienced, while Mandy felt the exact opposite. She had never competed in such an important pony show. She took a deep breath and tried to calm herself down by pretending she was just going on another trail ride. But her tummy felt like it was doing somersaults.

Faye must have noticed how Mandy was feeling. "You'll be fine," she assured her. "You're a really good rider."

"Don't forget, always keep one eye on the steward," Zach warned.

"And sit up straight. But look as if you're really comfortable," Faye instructed, checking the buckle on Jewel's girth.

"Like you're having the ride of your life," advised Zach. "And smile!"

Smile? Mandy swallowed hard. "I'll try." If she could smile during the class, she'd be in line for a best actress award! She stroked Jewel's neck. "I think you know more about it than I do," she told the pony. "I'm going to trust you to guide me."

"You've got to let her stride out with her neck arched," urged Zach.

Mrs. Nelson shook her head. "A word of advice now for you two," she said to the twins. "Stop bombarding poor Mandy! We know she'll do her best, and that's all we want."

"I guess," said Zach but Mandy could tell he desperately wanted Jewel to win.

There were fifteen minutes to go before their class, so there was time for Mandy and Jewel to warm up. With Faye leading the way in her wheelchair, Mandy rode to the practice area. Mrs. Nelson and Zach followed, Zach leaning on his mom's arm while he hopped along.

Jewel seemed relaxed when they entered the practice ring. She pricked up her ears as they trotted around, and Mandy started to relax, too.

But when the steward stood at the entrance to the main arena — the same one Jewel and Zach had competed in the other day — and called out, "Class twenty-one, Large Mountain and Moorland," Mandy felt her tummy start churning again. She looked at the blue sails around the arena, bulging like sails on a sailboat. Mandy took a deep breath. *We can do it,* she told herself. She leaned forward and stroked Jewel's neck. "You've learned so much this week and you've been amazing. Flags, plastic sheets, canvas, streamers — they can't hurt you. You just have to ignore them. You're the best horse here."

Even though Sea Cottage trotted past at that moment, Mandy meant every word.

Dr. Adam, Rollo, and Cara arrived just as Mandy was about to enter the ring. "What's going on?" said Dr. Adam when he saw Mandy in the saddle.

"It's a long story, Dad," she said. "We'll tell you later. Just wish us luck."

Dr. Adam raised both hands to show he had his fingers crossed. "You'll be great, sweetie." He smiled. "Both of you."

There were ten other ponies in the class. They all entered the ring and walked around the edge. Mandy tried to remember everything Zach and Faye had told her about Mountain and Moorland classes. *Sit up straight,* she reminded herself, aware that she was slouching a bit.

"Try to look more relaxed," whispered Faye when Mandy went past. She must have been overdoing the straight back!

Around the railing, the sails surged and sank and surged again, flapping noisily. Jewel didn't look at them, but her ears flicked back from time to time.

"They're only nylon sheets on a frame," Mandy whispered soothingly. She glanced at the steward in the center of the ring. He was pointing his whip at the lead pony, who broke into a trot and crossed the ring to the other corner.

Mandy and the others followed. After trotting around once more, they were ordered to canter.

"She looks great!" Faye called when Mandy went past.

At the steward's signal, the riders pulled their ponies up at the side of the ring. One by one, they were called into the center to perform their individual show. Sea Cottage was called out first, a dark bay Fell pony called Extra Time was second, and Mandy and Jewel sixth.

"Good luck," whispered the Loch Fyne team when Mandy walked Jewel into the middle. "You're doing great so far," Zach added. "Don't worry about the placings. They can all change at this stage."

Mandy walked and trotted Jewel in front of the judge, then cantered a neat figure eight and finished with a smooth gallop down the side of the ring. Bringing Jewel

to a halt, she felt like shouting for joy. Even with the advertising sails straining in the wind, the pony hadn't placed one foot wrong.

When Mrs. Nelson ran into the ring to help take off Jewel's saddle, she whispered, "You're both doing great. We could have a chance!" Mandy suddenly felt even more excited.

When Jewel was stripped out and standing with all four feet square, the judge came across to study her. She was a stern-faced woman dressed in a neat tweed suit. She reminded Mandy of a very strict teacher.

While the judge walked around Jewel, making notes on her clipboard, Mandy felt her knees turn to jelly. The woman's expression didn't change so there wasn't a hint of what she was thinking.

Finally, she came over to Mandy and Mrs. Nelson. "A good pony," she remarked. "Lovely clean lines and strong hindquarters."

Mandy wanted to cheer again. But she just said, "Of course. She's a Dales pony and they are bred to be strong."

"Hmph!" responded the judge and for a horrible moment, Mandy thought she was annoyed. But the smallest glimmer of a smile showed on the woman's face. "A Yorkshire girl, eh?" she said. "Now, will you lead the pony away and trot her back past me, please?"

At the end of the individual shows, the riders mounted and circled the ring again. A strong gust of wind came up and the advertising sails cracked and snapped. Jewel behaved perfectly.

Suddenly, there was another blast of wind. Out of the corner of her eye, Mandy saw a poster rip loose from a telegraph pole outside the ring. Her heart skipped a beat as the poster swirled through the air toward them. Jewel's ears flicked back. She had spotted it, too.

"It's OK," Mandy whispered, closing her legs against the pony's sides. She held the reins firmly, careful not to give the pony any signals to speed up.

The poster blew straight in front of Sea Cottage's legs. There was nothing his rider, a girl about Mandy's age, could have done to avoid it. Mandy watched in horror as the pony reared up, nearly unseating the startled girl.

In the middle of the ring, the judge frowned.

Mandy felt very sorry for the rider who clung on tightly, eventually managing to bring Sea Cottage under control. *I hope that doesn't count against her*, she thought, catching the girl's eye and giving her a friendly smile. Perhaps she'd try to find her after the class and share some flapping tips with her.

But the damage had been done. When the steward

started to call the riders in for the official placings, it wasn't Sea Cottage that was first, as so many must have expected.

"Extra Time!" the steward called, and the dark bay Fell pony went to the middle of the ring, his rider beaming from ear to ear. Mandy tried to imagine how it must feel to qualify for the championship. She was pleased for the stunning pony, but she also felt a stab of disappointment that it wasn't her and Jewel standing there. Still, they had done their best and that was what the Nelsons had wanted them to do.

"Loch Fyne Shining Jewel," the judge said next.

At first, Mandy didn't recognize the name. But a cheer from the Loch Fyne team brought her to her senses with a jolt. "That's us, Jewel!" she exclaimed. "We're second." Even though they wouldn't be going to the championship, it was a huge achievement to have done so well considering everything they'd been up against.

Mandy steered Jewel into place next to Extra Time. The judge came over with a red rosette and a white envelope that she gave to Mandy.

"What's this?" Mandy asked, turning the envelope over.

"Information about the championship," said the steward.

"You mean we've qualified, too?" she said, gasping.

"Of course. First and second go on to the big show." The steward smiled.

Stunned, Mandy looked across the ring. The Nelsons were hugging one another with joy, and her dad was smiling proudly. Rollo had his arm around Cara who raised her hand and gave Mandy a thumbs up.

Mandy stroked Jewel's neck. "You fabulous, fabulous pony," she said, feeling a lump rise in her throat.

The judge smiled warmly. "Well done, young lady," she said. "You showed the pony off beautifully. She's the best example of a Dales pony I've seen in a long time."

Mandy swallowed and concentrated on the red rosette that the judge was pinning on Jewel's bridle.

When all the ponies had been placed, it was time for a victory lap. As Mandy and Jewel cantered around the ring, the red ribbon streaming from the bridle, an enormous cheer went up from the crowd.

Mandy's smile couldn't have been wider. Jewel had completely conquered her fear. "You're not only a shining jewel," Mandy told her, leaning forward to give her a big hug. "You're the most precious one of all!"

ABOUT THE AUTHOR

Ben Baglio was born in New York, and grew up in a small town in southern New Jersey. He was the only boy in a family with three sisters.

Ben spent a lot of his childhood reading. English was always his favorite subject, and after graduating from high school, he went on to study English Literature at the University of Pennsylvania. During his coursework, he was able to spend a year in Edinburgh, Scotland.

After graduation, Ben worked as a children's book editor in New York City. He also wrote his first book, which was about the Olympics in ancient Greece. Five years later, he took a job at a publishing house in England.

Ben is the author of the Dolphin Diaries series, and is perhaps most well known for the Animal Ark and Animal Ark Hauntings series. These books were originally published in England (under the pseudonym Lucy Daniels), and have since gone on to be published in the U. S., and translated into 15 languages.

Aside from writing, Ben enjoys scuba diving and swimming, music and movies. He has a beagle named Bob, who is by his side whenever he writes.